Also by Valerie Hobbs

Stefan's Story

Sonny's War

Tender

Charlie's Run

Carolina Crow Girl

How Far Would You Have Gotten If I
Hadn't Called You Back?

Get It While It's Hot. Or Not.

This copy made possible by a generous
donation to the
Jackson County Library Foundation
from **Sherm and Wanda Olsrud.**

Letting go of Bobby James,
or how I found my self of steam

VALERIE HOBBS

Letting go of Bobby James, or how I found my self of steam

Frances Foster Books

Farrar Straus Giroux • New York

www.fsgkidsbooks.com

Library of Congress Cataloging-in-Publication Data
Hobbs, Valerie.
    Letting go of Bobby James, or how I found my self of steam / Valerie
Hobbs.— 1st ed.
        p.   cm.
    Summary: After being left by her husband at a gas station in Florida, sixteen-
year-old Sally Jo Walker, also known as Jody, makes some difficult decisions and
a better life for herself.
    ISBN 0-374-34384-5
    [1. Coming of age—Fiction.   2. Self-esteem—Fiction.   3. Wife abuse—
Fiction.   4. Florida—Fiction.]   I. Title: How I found my self of steam.
II. Title.

PZ7.H65237Le 2004
[Fic]—dc22

                                                                      2003056377

For Barbara

Letting go of Bobby James,
or how I found my self of steam

*D*ear Mr. Teeter,

This is about the coleslaw.

But first, I would like to take this opportunity to tell you how much we enjoyed the fine convenience of your food market in Perdido, Florida. Like I said to Bobby James (who wasn't in the greatest mood at the time), the coleslaw is probably just an oversight on your part. Still, I thought you'd want to hear about it. Bobby James said not to bother. An important personage like yourself would not take the time to read a letter from a plain old customer, he said.

That was when I showed him your color ad in the *Perdido News Press*. HARRIS TEETER IS WAITING TO HEAR FROM YOU! it said right there all bold. So I started in writing you about the coleslaw when the one thing led to another and left me (only sixteen years old) without a friend on the streets of Jackson Beach. It was none of it my fault as far as I can tell. Mostly I tried to keep Bobby James happy.

Which is something you have to do, married and all for just thirteen weeks and wanting to show my best like

Mama said. You have a new home now, Jody, she said, not really thinking too hard about it, 'cause we did not really have a home as yet. You got a new life now, she said. And that is true.

This is some country, isn't it? Born and raised in Purley like I was (that's Texas, too small for a Harris Teeter of your stature), when you get out on the road, well, it's a real eye-opener. The opportunities out there. I don't expect you and your missus do a lot of camping out, which is not to say that you do not enjoy the Great Outdoors, but what I picture is maybe a Hawaiian holiday in a Hilton hotel. Bobby James said what we had was a traveling Hilton, Bobby James's Duster (they stopped making the good Dusters, which Bobby James said was a big mistake. And if it's one thing Bobby James knows, it's cars). We had been staying in some of the prettiest campgrounds in the state of Florida. White sand, so white it hurts, and water just as blue as my mama's eyes. When we stopped the car in Perdido Beach to let Bobby's dogs out, I just shucked my shoes and made for the water. This is living, I said.

Bobby James says it's best to live one day at a time, which is what we were doing. Sometimes it got a little hard not knowing where we would stop, and no friends. But of course we had each other.

Do you remember a play by a Mr. Tennessee Williams? It's called *A Streetcar Named Desire*. That was our school play last year, which was a beautiful experience had by all. Remember Blanche, the flighty one? The one who believed in the kindness of strangers? Well, that's what I thought about that day in Perdido when we stopped at the Econo Gas and I wanted a cup of tea in the worst way. (Bobby James says tea drinking is putting on airs, but it isn't a highfalutin thing in our family, which has some English in it.) And when the lady said they didn't have tea, just drip coffee, I said that's all right, but then she looked at me in a special kind of knowing way and said she could open a box of Lipton from the shelf and make me a cup.

And she did, just like that.

Well, I could have cried, don't ask me why. There I was in the middle of a foreign state at the Econo and all, and some stranger really cares about a person like that, off the streets. Which is not what we were. I don't want to give you the wrong idea.

Florida is such a pretty place. You were right to put your stores down here. We passed so many new buildings, fancy apartment houses, stretched out along the beach, so close to the water you wonder how it is they don't fall in. We stopped and bought some shrimp off a fella by the side of the road. Two pounds, which was a splurge. And of course with shrimp, what you have got to have is coleslaw. It was time to find a market, of which yours is certainly the finest.

Bobby James would say this is none of anybody's business, which could be God's truth, but my mama always said, Jody, you have got the biggest mouth, which was supposed to shut me down but it never did. We got the shrimp cooked up and spread all out on a grocery bag (catsup and horseradish, $1.19 for the horseradish—maybe that was what did it, so much money for such a small bottle), and Bobby James is in one of his moods. He can be way up there one minute, which is when we fell in love, and the next minute he's lower than a swamp in a drought.

We are at a picnic table just an overhand pitch from the ocean, and the sun is shining something fierce. I'm about to give Bobby James a peck on the cheek because I'm feeling so good, when out of the blue he says something funny. As in funny peculiar. Just why did I want to get hitched up with him anyway? he asks. And I can see he doesn't really want the answer, and he's starting to heat up the way he does. What you need to do then is play him out on a long line and wait till he can be reeled back in. But this time he winds up tighter and tighter, and then he just pops me.

Just like that, with the back of his hand.

And some voice inside tells me not to cry out, some voice that's been there all the while I guess, just waiting for the right time. And the bright blue ocean and that pretty white sand and the kids streaking by on their skateboards and the family right next to us in the silver RV all tip away and for a minute go black.

Popped me winded.

What could I say? I have never in my life had a hand laid on me. Spoiled, by some accounts, but without a daddy around enough to keep me in line, maybe I just grew up, well, like a tree or a stalk of corn, left alone to go my own way. I look at Bobby James and out at the clear blue ocean and back at Bobby James, and Bobby James looks at me, his eyes gone wild but simmering down some, and I can see we have reached some kind of a place that we can never go back from. But it is a hard thing to put into words.

Which is why I started this letter.

I don't want you to get Bobby James wrong. He has the biggest heart, everybody says so. Things were great when Purley had the oil, but when it was gone, well, there wasn't much left for a man to do.

Mr. Teeter, I know just what you are thinking. Why would a girl of some intelligence (first in all my family to graduate eighth grade) marry a boy with such small prospects? But you don't know Bobby James. The first time I saw him, which was Patsy Cline Night at the rec center, I said he's for me. I know it's just a girl's foolishness but he has the most beautiful smile and he was smiling a lot that night, the girls hanging around him like mayflies. But after a while he's looking my way and I can't hardly believe it. Me with my hair all gone out of its curl and hanging like it does in the heat, and without a figure to speak of. But then Bobby James is coming right through the crowd, like Fate, and I am in his arms dancing.

The way we came together, it was perfect. Like no matter what happened after, I would never feel that way ever again with anybody else. I wonder sometimes how it is that a thing can feel so right and be so wrong?

In the morning, I take a good hard look at this face in the mirror of the Econo ladies' and I say, Jody, just do the best with what the good Lord gave you, which is advice I always try to follow, no matter what. And so there I am with my hair all done up in sponge rollers and putting on some makeup to match the one eye to the other, when Bobby James bangs on the door. We ain't got all day, he says, which is funny because of course that is all we *have* got. I say, In a minute, but I can't get the eye right, puffy and closed up like it is. Hurry up in there, Bobby James says, I'm not waiting around all day. But I work and I work at this face, and then I take out my rollers, and after a while he stops knocking.

Sometimes what you're feeling inside makes a lot more sense than what your outside's doing, if you know what I mean.

Once, I heard the Duster's horn. It sounded far away, like an echo in a shell.

Sorry I got off the track. What I meant to do right off was to give you a genuine, down-home, Purley, Texas, recipe for coleslaw and I almost forgot. If I may say so, yours could use improvement. I apologize for the paper towel, which is all I could find to write on. You will have to figure out how to make it, the coleslaw that is, in the big batches.

Down-Home Coleslaw

1 head fresh green cabbage (if you can push your
   finger into it, it is not fresh)
1 small head red cabbage, also fresh

1/2 cup mayo (this is the part where you overdo it!)

1/2 cup apple cider vinegar

Salt and pepper

A scattering of poppy seeds (with a light hand, like a
blessing)

Yours truly,
Mrs. Sally Jo Walker (Jody)

October 4, 1991

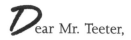ear Mr. Teeter,

Remember the ladies' room? Well, I stayed in there about as long as anybody ever stayed in a ladies' when they didn't have to. Every now and again the doorknob would rattle, some poor lady needing to use the facilities, and bad as I felt for hogging the place, I surely could not face my Fate.

Outside that door was Bobby James waiting, his fists stuffed down into the pockets of his Wranglers and his face all heated up the way it gets. Or there was nothing at all, a whole wide world with nobody but strangers in it.

Which was worse, I did not know.

This is where Willie Nelson comes in, the world-famous country singer? His words would not leave my mind be: "Forgiving you is easy," Willy said, "but forgetting seems to take the longest time." I just kept staring at my sorry face and my right eye that kept on crying even when I wasn't. With all my heart, I loved Bobby James Walker. I forgave him, too. But I did not want to see him anymore. Not then, and maybe not ever.

You just had to wonder, standing there. Would you

thank Willie someday for the words that kept you in the ladies' way past the limit of Bobby James's patience? Or would you just be sorry that you had ever bought his greatest hits on tape?

I read the sign on the back of the door that said to wash your hands in the Spanish language a couple of times. Then I took a real deep breath and turned the knob.

No Bobby James.

I snuck around the cans of stacked-up Pennzoil and peeked down the row of chips and crackers, dips and spreads.

No Bobby James.

Then I remembered the magazines. He always had to have his *Car and Driver*. But there was only a couple little fellas sneaking peeks at a girlie magazine.

PINEAPPLE SLURPEES 99¢ said a sign in hurtful yellow letters all across the window. I had to get out of there.

Outside, everything was clear and bright, like a fever dream. Butterflies, the sick kind, flew into my stomach. My head spun me dizzy. Sitting on the curb, I looked out at the world without Bobby James in it. Hot tar and gasoline, fleas biting on my ankles.

Now what have you done, said that little voice inside, what have you gone and done now?

Cars kept driving in from the highway, getting their gas and leaving like it was any other day. I could not believe it. Not a one was a Duster.

What was my life without Bobby James in it?

I waited for the longest time, thinking he'd come back,

grinning like he'd played the best trick. That grin could turn me right around; I knew it could. He knew it, too. He'd get out of the Duster to let me get in, the right door stuck like it is from the dent. I would climb inside like nothing had happened.

Except that it did.

I thought some about calling Mama, wondering what she would say. But I already knew. Honor your vows, she would tell me, especially the for-worst part, which was right now. She'd endured a whole lot more from Daddy over the years and was still holding on. It's what you do. Standing there hugging my drawstring bag with all I had left in the world inside it, I thought about life in Purley—how it was and how it would always be. I thought a long while about going home.

As far as I could get myself to go was the bus stop.

In case you have ever wondered—from the inside, riding the bus in Florida is like riding the bus anywhere. Just plain people. Dark faces, light faces, old people clinging to their lives like plastic wrap. Young ones, too, bumping down the aisle with backpacks and skateboards, closed in by the music stuck to their ears. Then there's the folks riding the whole day long because it's what they know to do. All in all, good, decent people, like anywhere, trying to make their way.

Nothing to be scared of, Jody, says I. Nothing to fear but fear itself, which is what a famous president said, and he should know.

I found me a seat near the back where I could hide my

bad eye to the side and watch the scenery, a wonder to behold. Palm trees swaying tall as the First Commerce Bank in Dallas, the sky behind a sort of washed-out blue. There's no sky anywhere like the blue sky in Texas, a known fact. Still, what sights there are to see.

Would you believe, an alligator! Right there by the roadside. Of course, nobody but me pays the critter any mind. That old gray gator's taking his sweet time, lifting one big claw, then thinking a while before putting it down, his long bumpy snout swaying low to the ground. Well, the chills just shot all down my back. Was that gator a Sign? Was I heading into danger far greater than what I had left behind?

The thing is, I was not going home. What I was up to that first day, filled to the brim with my bravest, scaredest self, was shopping for a new home in which to begin my future.

I say this with a sorry heart, Mr. Teeter, knowing that before God and our assembled loved ones I had promised myself—soul and body, till death do us part—to a Walker. I am not ready to be any person's wife. When Bobby James and I went cruising down that straight white Florida highway, swimming-pool blue water on both sides stretched far as you could see? Well, I could breathe. I felt my heart escaping right out the window and pulling me along with it, like the string end of a kite.

Life is too short to suffer anybody's meanness, which is what you can learn eating shrimp with store-bought coleslaw, if you look it straight in the face.

But where was there to go? And how would I know it when I got there? I kept watching out the window for a beach, but Florida is not all pretty beaches, sad to say. After a while, the heat and the drone of that bus engine knocked me out and I started in to dreaming. I dreamed about rocking on my mama's sweet shoulder, like I was a baby again. I woke up to the great surprise of my head in a perfect stranger's lap.

I jumped right up, sorry every which way.

"Not to worry, child," said the plus-size lady. The wrinkles on her face were all going the right way, like her life was exactly the way she wanted it. "You just put your head back down if you want. I'll wake you when we get there."

Sleeping in a Duster with Pete and Repeat, Bobby's dogs, all those weeks must have taken its toll on me. I could not stop my head from dropping back down onto that nice padded lap, while the highway went along, with scenery you could sleep through and not miss a thing.

The hiss of bus brakes woke me up.

"Here we are," the lady said, gathering up her bags. "Jackson Beach. It's the last stop."

I looked out the window and what did I see but a Harris Teeter. It made me feel good, I don't know why. I guess, because you were the one person in all of that state that knew me.

The lady gathered all her bags and got up. Then she gave me a look straight on. "You get you some ice on that eye, you hear?"

It was like she knew the whole story without me saying a thing.

"I will," I said.

She stood there for another minute like there was something else hanging on to her mind. Then she shuffled down the aisle and out the door with all the other folks.

And so did I.

*W*ell, I had to check the coleslaw first off. Sure enough, same as the one you make in Perdido with the too much mayo. Sometimes a person almost wants to be wrong.

I purchased a box of doughnuts, your white flour items being cheaper than the rest, and a small size milk. After that bus fare, all the money to my name was in my curler case folded eight ways.

This is what I mean by not being ready. A good wife would have turned all she had over to her husband, like my mama always did. Most of it anyway. But how could I forget how a nickel here, a dime there ended up with me having the prettiest sunflower-yellow graduation dress when it never could have been otherwise. That last couple of minutes in Purley, Bobby James gunning the engine, cans all tied to the bumper and shoe polish on the back window proclaiming for all to see, I remembered Mama's blue-and-white sugar bowl with the egg money in it, and quick tucked away a twenty-dollar bill.

At the register, the cashier lady had a time pulling that twenty out of my hand. How could she know it was all I had to keep body and soul together until gainfilled employment could be found?

After two doughnuts and half the milk, I got right to work on that.

"Sorry," said Popeye's.

"Nope," said Hardee's.

"Try next week," said Sonny's Barbecue.

I would have tried you, Mr. Teeter, but I was not looking my best.

By nightfall, I had worn a hole in my sandal big as the one in my heart. But there was a beach, and so I had my supper there, sitting in the sand.

The moon was nothing more than a hangnail in a coal black sky. Hugging my knees, I tried not to think of the next thing, which was a place to sleep. Lights were glowing out onto the sand from the Sea Horse Motel. Imagine what a room in there was like! All pink and green, with sea horse paintings and HBO for free. You could probably pick up the telephone and call for your dinner, anything you wanted. Put it on the bill, you would say.

Or you could just dig yourself a pit right there in the sand with all your fancy thinking.

I got up and brushed myself off. What I needed was a nice green park with grass.

Even with the doughnut box cardboard over the hole in my sandal, it was some hard walking. Not a clump of grass anywhere. The farther I went, the scarier the streets got, with broken-down cars, dog poop, and chain-link fences, which was a good thing because of all the dogs. Somebody kept walking behind me, crunching on glass, but when I turned to see, they were always gone. I started walking real fast, and then I was running.

After a while, all out of breath, I came to a place I could breathe in. Here was all the grass anybody could want, only every bit was on somebody's lawn. Soft-looking streetlights shone down, making leaf shadows on the sidewalk.

Well, it was all so beautiful it broke you right down. Never in my entire sixteen years of living had I felt like life was winning this bad against me.

The street was so quiet. Slap, slap, went my broken down sandal. Then slower and slower. I stopped to lean on a car to rest. It was a nice little car without a speck of dirt on it. I ran my hand over the smooth top. Well, then one thing sort of led to another. I opened the back door and crawled in.

Real quick, I locked all the doors. Then I waited with my heart knocking for a light to come on in the house across the dark lawn.

Nothing. Just the quiet. Some fireflies winking. There had to be a law about sleeping in other people's cars, a law that I was breaking that very minute. Life had turned me into a criminal in less than one day.

I laid myself down on that little seat with my knees up to my chin, which is when I had the thought that criminals are sure to get. If I was going to pick a car anyway, why not a big fancy one?

Thoughts like that one will keep you awake no matter how weary your soul is. But the seat was like marshmallow and I must have slept some, as I awoke at dawn to the banging and screeching of a garbage truck. After the truck passed, I slipped out of the car and ran a whole three blocks without once looking back.

Mr. Teeter, if I was the president, what I would do first is give out free showers. A person just doesn't have the heart to go on if she needs a bath even more than she needs a good breakfast.

I cleaned up at a mini-mart as best I could with a paper towel and that smelly yellow soap. My hair was the worst part. Hanging limp like that made my eye look sadder than it already was. This is when you start to think about sunglasses, the wraparound kind.

Well, there they were, the minute I stepped outside the ladies' all stacked on a turn stand—$5.99 for any pair you wanted. A fortune. I put some on, just to try them. Then I poured a cup of coffee, the large size, and filled it half up with milk.

"Dollar six," said the girl at the counter.

Well, I knew that didn't pay for the sunglasses. Still, I stood there for the longest time biting my tongue, too long for a really decent person. "Um, how much for these?" I said, setting the glasses down on the counter.

That girl? She took one long hard look at my eye and my mussed-up clothes. "Go on," she said, like she was mad but not really? "They're on the house."

I could hardly believe my ears. "You sure?"

"I said go on." She shot her head toward the door. "Get on out of here."

Half the day, I searched for employment. At last, when hope was near lost, there in the window of Thelma's Open 24-Hour Café and Grill was a handmade sign: HELP WANTED.

This is your chance, Jody, says I. Make the best of it. I took off my sunglasses, because you have to with a job, and went inside.

*T*helma's Open 24-Hour Café and Grill is the kind of place that used to be homey, with ducks swimming on the wallpaper and red plastic booths for people to gather in. But hard times had come upon it, and everything looked done in. A couple of sour-faced customers sat at the counter, fanning themselves with the menus. In the back, a swamp cooler churned away. It hardly did a thing but stir that little ribbon around.

Miss Thelma was at the register. I did not know she was Miss Thelma at first, but as she was counting money I put two and two together and inquired about the job.

Miss Thelma kept counting.

"Excuse me," I said, watching the ash from the cigarette stuck in her mouth get longer and longer. "Is the job already taken?"

"Quit'cher yammerin'," she said. "I am losing my count. Go sit."

And so I did. It took the longest time for that ash to fall.

The Jackson Beach Funerals and Monuments calendar stuck to the wall behind Miss Thelma was a month behind. I watched her knobby fingers scratch up every coin before, at long last, she looked up. She squinched her eyes at me, I hoped for lack of eyesight, as I was a good deal more presentable than I would be in the days to come.

While Miss Thelma was counting, I had spit-rubbed the only real bad spot on my jeans skirt, thinking sadly of my true-so with the three brand-new skirt-and-top sets sitting in my bungee-wrapped suitcase in the trunk of the Duster.

I guess I didn't look too bad after all, because Miss Thelma came around the counter waving an employment form.

"Who did your eye like that?" she said.

I couldn't look her straight on. "Took a bad fall," I said.

"You the clumsy type?"

"No, ma'am."

She pushed the form at me, along with a wore-down pencil.   .

My daddy, who never said one good thing about anybody, said this one good thing about me. I could always think on my feet. As Miss Thelma tapped her fingernails on the tabletop, I wrote every bit of the truth that needed to stretch if I was to survive from that day forward, and I did it in a good steady hand.

Miss Thelma scarcely glanced it over. "You'll do," she said, and pushed me along into the kitchen, thumping her cane as she went.

What greeted me was a sight: dishes coated with egg scum and bacon grease stacked to the ceiling, where flypaper dangled down, black with stuck flies. The garbage pail was missing a lid. It was filled with hog slop and more flies. A long parade of roaches went straight up the wall behind the sink and into a hole in the ceiling.

It made your stomach kind of wash out from under you. But I got right to work.

A good while later, I had finished that pile of dishes with only a finger cut to show for it.

Miss Thelma, who only takes the money, gave me a Band-Aid and left me to wrap it myself, which is always hard with fingers. So I asked Marilyn, the head waitress, who is just as nice as Miss Thelma is mean. But sad in that same way. I did not believe the two were related by blood, however, as Marilyn was plump as a good Easter hen with a head of orange curls tied up like I Love Lucy.

It was Marilyn, and not Miss Thelma, who told me to order a meal. It had to be from the lunch side of the menu, $4.99 if you paid for it, no substitutions. I ate every bite of that chicken-fried steak like it was my last meal on this earth.

Miss Thelma paid me straight out of the register, which she probably would not have if she knew she was saving my life. But she was only saving herself the trouble of paying taxes on me. I collected my first day's hard-earned wages, three dollars of it in pennies and nickels, which weighed me down some.

"You gonna be back tomorrow?" Miss Thelma said. You could tell she was the type that wouldn't trust a Bible salesman.

"Yes, ma'am," I said, polite as you please. "And every day after that you need me."

"Hmmmph," she said, which meant I don't know what. "Ma'am?"

She looked up, squinty-eyed and mean-looking.

"I could sure use some rubber gloves," I said. My hands were a sight, all puffy and red from the steamy hot water.

"We don't supply them," she said, like she was sucking on a pickle chip. "Get some at the Walgreens. And get you a Goody hair net while you're at it."

Outside, there were just the three choices to make. Left, right, or straight ahead. The lights were brighter to the left, where a movie house was, so I went that way.

The cineplex was showing a picture called The Silence of the Lambs, PG by the sound of it, with Jodie Foster, my namesake. I thought how nice it would be to sit back, forget my troubles, and watch a movie about lambs. But I would only be putting off what I knew must be taken care of before too long: finding another place to sleep the night.

When I was just a youngster, I'd run away from home every chance I got. Out there in the big wide world all on my own, I could do anything I wanted. Make a camp, fish, write in my private diary. I would dream about going all around the world in a hot-air balloon. I thought I was pretty big stuff, which is how you think not half a mile from your own front door.

I didn't feel like big stuff anymore.

I set off walking.

Gas stations, mini-marts, vacant lots, killer vans, a pack of boys with no good on their minds that I could see, smoking cigarettes. With each step, my spirits sank lower.

Not a tree, not a park bench, no place to crawl under. Like a dog trying to settle down for a good rest, I had walked myself in circles.

And there I was back at the cineplex again, which could only be a Sign, as there was nobody guarding the door or the ticket booth either. I snuck right in, past the popcorn-and-candy stand, where backs were turned, and into the darkened theater.

The movie was not what I had thought. It was the kind you have to close your eyes for, or else be ready to suffer the consequences. From all the dishes, I was tired enough to conk right out. Trouble was, I could still hear, and what went on behind my eyelids was almost worse than what was on the screen.

I settled for keeping one eye open. That way, I could watch for the usher in case he had counted heads and found an extra one. And I would only see about half the movie.

When I had endured the thing almost to the end, I got up and headed for the ladies'.

Well, the mirror in there was the truth-telling kind. It made you wonder if a female had anything to do with the building of the cineplex—probably not. I washed up best I could and brushed my teeth with my travel toothbrush.

It was in a stall that Fate stepped in once again. I heard the ladies' door open.

"Anybody in here?" came a voice. "Anybody here?"

I heard some metal banging, then the swish of water and the wringing of a mop. I lifted my feet, my heart beating like a monkey with a drum, while whoever it was mopped that floor without once going near the commodes, a real sloppy job. Then the lights went out and the door sighed to a close.

There in the stall, I waited the longest time, rolling my hair by feel. But I couldn't stay sitting on a toilet seat forever. Sticking my hands out like blindman's buff, I found my way across the floor to the door and peeked out.

It was dark there, too. Not as dark as in the ladies', but with that feeling you always get when nobody's home. Inside the theater, the curtains were pulled and all the seats were empty. Listening to my own self breathe, I went down the aisle, popcorn crunching under my feet loud as popping balloons. If somebody was anywhere near, I was going to be caught for sure.

I picked a seat close to the front. From there, I figured I could make a run for the exit if I had to.

Then I thought better of that plan. Any old person could come through that exit, a rapist or ax murderer, how did I know?

I went to the back instead, where every shadow looked like something coming out of a grave. I could not settle down. Just about the time my eyes got heavy, I'd hear some scratching, then some scurrying around.

Whole families of mice set up house in the movies after they think we're all gone. If you want to get some sleep, you have to keep your feet up the whole time.

Word to the wise.

I thought about all those years at home when I wanted

my own bed, instead of the little part the twins didn't hog, and how lucky you are for just a piece of something sometimes.

I woke up to the sound of my stomach going crazy from having nothing in it but the memory of chicken-fried steak. After washing up and doing my hair and face, I walked into the lobby big as you please, like an actress on a coffee break. But when I thought to eat the leftover popcorn for free, my conscience made me leave fifty-five cents, the small-bag price.

After that, I went back into the theater and out the back exit. Holding the door with my foot, I unwrapped the Band-Aid from my finger. It had just enough stick left to keep that door from closing all the way.

It wasn't exactly a home, but it wasn't a car either. I had moved up in the world in only one day.

*M*ama says that a resourceful person always knows what to do with her free time, so I set off in search of a library and found a lake instead. Jackson Lake was about the prettiest place you ever saw. All across, the water rippled gold and weeping willows hung down, reminding me once again of my mama, as they are her favorite trees.

I found a bench and sat down.

That was when the misgivings began to cloud my head like gnats at a church picnic. Had I made the biggest mistake letting Bobby James go? It was only the one slap, and then a promise after a while that he would never, ever lay a hand on me again. Well, forgive and forget, I said. What kind of a person would turn down a heartfelt apology, more or less?

What did I have without Bobby James? Only a dishwasher job and a seat in a movie house. It was crazy what I was doing. Bus fare back to Purley wouldn't cost near what rent would in a place like Jackson Beach. In Purley, I could set up house as a lawful wedded wife. Once we got a house, that is. But Bobby James's mama liked me well enough. We could make a go of it there if we had to.

You wouldn't be all alone, Jody, said I. Only two days and already I was talking to myself out loud.

Down by the lake, some families were feeding a pack of greedy ducks, the kind we'd have shot and ate in Purley. One lady snatched up her baby as a stupid goose went honking after it on a dead run. I thought about how I wanted a family of my own someday, but not with a person who could not rein his temper in, no more than a goose could.

In the sunshine you could see how my skirt was covered all around the bottom with just about everything on Miss Thelma's menu. The aprons only went that far down. Well, as there is nothing like a shopping trip to lift the spirits, I set my worries aside and headed into town.

HACIENDA THRIFT SHOP, said the sign, MEN'S SHIRTS HALF OFF. It wasn't the best day, but I went inside anyway.

My arms were full in no time, which was not so good. My heart was set on a pair of brand-name jeans in perfect shape, but they were twice what they'd have set me back in Purley. T-shirts were $1.99 each, but the girl is not yet born who can get by with a single shirt.

Hoping they would still be there when I had some more money, I hid a pair of khaki slacks in with the drapes, the oldest trick in the book.

Shoes were next. This is always the hard find, as people only part with the ones that pinch. But I found some blue Keds that wouldn't show the dirt, and thanked my lucky stars when they were only about one size too big.

Well, I would not be a normal person if unmentionables

did not come to mind. Washing out my one set every single night at the cineplex was going to be a chore, but you have to draw your line at the thrift store and that's where I draw mine.

The girl cashier was about my age and in the family way. Black stringy hair. Pea green eye shadow. Skin pale as milk. No ring.

"I'm real pleased with these jeans," I said, passing them over, making pleasant conversation the way you do. "I don't think they got wore even once."

"Uh-huh," she said, punching buttons on the register. What was with all the sad sacks in Jackson Beach? Here was a girl with her whole life in front of her, and a decent job to boot, but could she give a person the time of day? No.

"Not too busy yet, huh?" I said.

"Nuh-uh." She punched some buttons, then some more. The register buzzed but the drawer didn't pop. "Crap!" she yelled, snatching back her fingers as if they got burned. "I did it again. It won't open!" She tried every last button, going straight down the rows, getting more and more worked up with every punch.

"Maybe you could start all over again," I said, in a calm voice. "Do a void." Where I picked that up I will never know, but the girl went right on punching, her pale face taking on some welcome color.

"What the double hell are you doing?" This older man with Scotch-taped glasses came huffing out of the back.

"Can't you do a simple sale yet? Here! Get away from there." He nudged the girl aside and took over, bagging my purchases and handing me some money back. "Have a nice day," he said, changing his tune like a leopard changes his spots.

My stomach felt loose, as if it was me being yelled at instead of that poor girl. I tried catching her eye as I went out, but she was looking right through me as if I wasn't there, lost in a pit of misery.

It was hard not to dwell upon the plight of the common person as I made my way toward Thelma's. The fairness of things, or the unfairness, more like. This was what I thought. What if our president up and decided to share all the money so that everybody got the same? It was a simple idea from, Lord knows, a simple mind but no worse than the one they use now that makes people live in doorways. You probably think that share and share alike isn't good for business, but the face of misery is one you can never forget.

And to beat all, I saw that very same face again that very same day.

Why Miss Thelma didn't have me start until eleven o'clock was hard to figure out as, once again, I faced Dish Mountain. Didn't she know that egg scum sticks hard as glue in no time flat if you don't scrape it right off? And here it was, four hours later.

I filled the sink with hot soapy water, wishing that, at

the very rock-bottom least, people had the good sense not to stub their cigarette butts into their egg scum. I put on my rubber gloves and my Goody hair net and dug in.

Lucky for me, Thelma's Open 24-Hour Café and Grill wasn't open twenty-four hours. Still, it made you wonder why they never changed the sign.

About halfway through that pile, I took a break. When I came out of the back bathroom, there was Miss Thelma at the sink, leaning on her cane. "Dishwater ain't hot enough," she said, and cranked the hot full blast. "Where's the scrubber? You got to use the scrubber."

Well, I said, I didn't know there was one.

"Of course there's one," she said. "There's always a scrubber. Anybody with a lick of sense . . ." She went thumping off to find a scrubber or maybe just to count her money, as the scrubber didn't turn up until the next day, which when it did made the job a good deal easier.

Doing those dishes was like chopping the heads off dragons. I'd wash one plate and three more would turn up. It wasn't until 2:30 p.m. that I saw myself clear. By then I was shaking all over from hunger.

I went out the swinging door into the café. Miss Thelma was nowhere in sight. "She's gone home," Marilyn said, catching a look in my face. "She's working a split. Order what you want from the menu. I won't tell."

I took her at her word and ordered up a mess of scrambled eggs, bacon, home fries, and white toast. Enrique, the cook, said not one thing about it, and Marilyn delivered my plate like I was a regular paying customer.

Then she poured herself a cup of coffee and plunked down across from me. "Don't you let Thelma get you down, hon," she said, her sad brown eyes so kind. "She's just upset because her son took a one-week vacation. The first in years! He's the manager. Loves balloons, the ones with the hot air, so he went to that big show in Arizona. When he comes back, the old lady won't be around near as much."

Hot-air balloons! Who would have thought? It had to be a Sign.

"So what brings you to Jackson Beach?" Marilyn lit up. Then she flapped her hand through the smoke to send it off. She was settling in for a talk the way good country people do, letting their hair down. It was an invitation too tempting to decline. When I got to the part about Bobby James and the dirty Econo ladies', Marilyn cupped her hand right over mine and leaned across the table. "You did the right thing, Jody," she said. "Don't you never doubt it. A man who hits a woman once will do it again, mark my words. It's just a matter of time."

She sighed, looking down at her hand with the pearl ring, brushing off some ash. That sigh said it all.

"Did you . . . Were you . . . ?" It didn't feel right to ask, her being older, but she did not mind one bit.

When she was through telling me about the boyfriends and the husbands and the daughter killed by a drunk driver, I said to myself, Jody, you have one easy time of it and don't you never forget it.

No dishes came in between then and the start of dinner,

but when I heard the thump of Miss Thelma's cane I was glad to be under the sink scraping gum off the floor with a butter knife. She stood there doing who knows what, then she thumped on out, leaving me be.

It was a slow night of business. I stuck my head out to see what might be coming in, but a steady rain was falling outside and the café was empty except for Phyliss, the night waitress, an older lady with a hitch in her gitalong that slowed her down some on the busy nights.

A policeman was sipping coffee at the counter.

Then who comes through the door but the girl from the thrift store, soaked, black hair stringing down, and her belly punched right out in front of a wet man's T-shirt. The policeman glances over and turns back to his coffee. The girl slides into a booth, pushing her hair back off her face, and stares out the window, chin on her palm. I don't have to see her face to know what is on it. She is one mournful creature. I grab up a dish towel, glad that Miss Thelma isn't there to witness it, and take it on over to the girl.

"Here," I say. "Dry off."

She looks at me suspicious, like I'm trying to get something from her instead of the other way around. "Thanks," she says, taking the towel and drying off as best she can. "I'll have a cup of coffee."

Like I'd been doing it all my life, I pour the girl a cup of coffee and take it on over to her without spilling one drop. Her face is warmed-over death itself. "You all right?"

She gives me that scared-animal look. "Yeah, why?"

"Remember me? I'm the one you waited on this morning when the register wouldn't work."

"Oh. Yeah." She looks back out the window, at the rain sliding down. "Seems like a week ago already." She blows across the coffee to cool it down some. "I got fired."

I tell her that I'm sorry for her loss.

She shrugs. "It's not the first time."

I stick out my hand. "Name's Jody. Nice to meet you."

She looks at my hand before she takes it and does the dead-fish shake. "Effaline," she says.

"Well, my birth name is Sally Jo. Jody is what stuck, though."

"You new here?"

"Brand-new."

"Thought so. New in town, too, right?"

I shrug. "Yeah."

"Thought so. That job sign goes in the window every couple weeks. Nobody stays. Don't know why."

I did, but unpleasant as Miss Thelma was, she was still my boss, so I keep my mouth shut.

Effaline blows her nose in a napkin. Her eyes are eerie looking, with nearly all the blue rinsed out of them, pea green eye shadow all around. "Where ya living?"

I nod my head toward the cineplex. "Down there a ways."

"Apartment? Duplex? What?"

I could almost feel that policeman listening in from the counter with his super-radar ears. "Well, it isn't a place I'm staying for long," I say, instead of the whole truth, which she doesn't have to know.

"I got to find a place," she says. "I'm staying over at Sandyland Apartments, but . . ." She shrugs, looks back out the window.

Phyliss comes over with the coffeepot. "Got caught in the rain, huh?" She fills Effaline's coffee cup and moves on, her big hips rolling. I check the clock. To my surprise, I am already off.

"Nice to meet you, Effaline," I say. "I'll take that towel back now."

"What? Oh, yeah." She hands it over. "Thanks. I never leave a tip, but don't take it personally, okay? I'm a little low on funds."

"It's not my job anyway," I say. "I'm just the dish-washer."

"I know," she says. "It's the job nobody wants."

I tell Phyliss I'm fixing to leave.

"That girl?" she says in a hushed voice, nodding her head at Effaline. "She's been in here every night for the past three weeks. Sits there staring out the window, drinking up all the coffee. If you ask me, she's in some kind of trouble."

"About eight months' worth by the looks of it."

"Yeah. Not married either." She clucks her tongue.

Phyliss is still shaking her head and clucking as I head for the door.

"Miz Bussard left your pay in a envelope up by the reg-ister."

Well, there I am again, about to cry, and for no reason

but normal human kindness. It was stuck way down in Miss Thelma Bussard's heart like anybody else's heart. She just didn't want anybody to know it was there.

Did you ever wonder what happens to all the homeless people in the rain? Where they go? Well, I surely did as I hopped puddles on my way to the cineplex with the *Jackson Beach Sun Times* for an umbrella. Dark thoughts flew at me like a nasty pack of blackbirds. What if my Band-Aid trick didn't work? What if I couldn't sneak into the cineplex? What if I got kicked out once I got in there? Where would I sleep in the rain?

For the umpteenth time since leaving Bobby James, I heard my mind asking what in the world did I think I was doing. Inside, the shaky little light of hope I'd been carrying went dim. I was just a runaway with nothing more to my name than the job nobody wanted. From here, up looked like a long, long way.

*I*t's all the little things that help a person through the pits of life. The movie had changed! No more Mr. Fava Beans, no more worrying about Clarice, who I could only see as Jodie Foster, my namesake, getting killed or worse.

But, first, all was lost. The cineplex back door was shut tight, my Band-Aid sitting in a puddle. I ran through the rain to the front. Two fellas stood blocking the door. The one in the white shirt I took for the usher. The one in the suit I figured for the boss, because his mouth kept going the whole time, along with his teaching finger. The poor fella in the white shirt kept nodding his head like a spring-headed doll on a dashboard.

I was soaked clean through by the time a side door opened and people came ducking out through the rain. I slipped in and went right to the ladies', wishing that I'd had the good sense to buy me a towel instead of those brand-name jeans.

As hair is being let down here, I should tell you that the towels from the linen supply stacked so neat on Thelma's shelf were like Eve's apples to me. But as I did not want a snake in my garden, I bought myself a towel the first chance I got.

The movie was almost full but I found a seat in my same place. This one started out okay, but before long was chopping the legs off people. Misery, it was called, and if you thought for a month, you could not think up a better title. Here was this regular book writer who wrecks his car through no fault of his own and ends up tied to the bed of a strapping woman, who is his biggest fan, according to her. A story like that takes a stronger stomach than what I've got to watch clear through. I went back to the ladies', where I wrote a letter to Mama, using a folded place mat from Thelma's, which was not exactly stealing as it was only paper.

Now this was a hard thing, not only because my pen needed a good shaking about every couple of words to get the ink down. I could see clear as day my poor mama reading my words in the light of the kitchen window. One hand would be over her heart as she learned how I had been cruelly abandoned practically at the altar and had decided, after some hard thinking, to pursue my future elsewhere.

The slap is a thing I left out, knowing it would plain break her heart. Two nights and two movies at the cineplex told a person, if she didn't already know it, that misery was already loose in the world and did not need me adding to it.

What with the stopping and starting, the sighing and

sniffing, it took me as long to write that letter as it took the person to write that terrible movie. At the very minute I signed my name, the ladies' filled right up with a line at the door. I hung around acting normal as I could until the last was gone. Then I went into a stall to hold up my feet and wait.

Sure enough, before long comes the floor washer. "Anybody in here? Anybody here?"

Knowing that the toilets got done on the day shift would have saved me that sick feeling you get when you are about to be caught and punished. But this was something I did not learn until it didn't matter anymore.

When the floor mopper left, I brushed my teeth and rolled my hair without the water, as it was still damp from the rain. My makeup had all washed off, and the bad eye stuck out like a ripe purple plum. But a new kind of look was in the good one that said I'd grown up some in my two days of being all alone in the world. Even if I had the job nobody wanted, it was a job.

I went back out into the empty theater, settled into my seat, pushed it back as far as it would go. I had never been so dog-tired in all my life.

"Hey! Hey!" Something was poking at my shoulder. "Hey, you got to wake up!"

I open my eyes. A round white face with squinty eyes hangs down over mine like the moon. "It's morning. The movie doesn't play in the morning."

I sit bolt upright, scaring the fella a little, as he jumps back and starts wringing his chubby white hands together. "You're not supposed to be here now."

I stand up. My full height does not come near to matching him. "That movie put me right to sleep," I say, all in a huff. "You shouldn't show such boring movies!"

That big old boy keeps looking like he wants to sweep me right up the aisle with his broom and out the door. "You got to go. You can't be in here. You got to go now."

I grab my drawstring bag and the Hacienda bag that I'm using for my clothes. "I'm leaving, I'm leaving. Hold your horses."

Halfway up the aisle, I whip around and there he is, breathing down my neck. He follows me all the way outside and when I turn the corner, there he is watching, his round face resting on his hands atop that broom handle.

The library was a welcome sight when at last I found it, homey and small. Peppertrees all around to make a lacy shade. Inside was that papery dusty smell all libraries get to have. Movie theaters and gas-station bathrooms and kitchens in open-24-hour cafés all have their own personal smell you would know with your eyes closed. The same can be said for libraries. Only the library smell is a whole lot better.

In my wallet was my Purley Public Library card. I didn't figure it would work here, but it showed I was an upstanding person at least.

"My. All the way from Texas," the library lady said, pushing my card back across the counter. "Did you move here with family?"

Was that a fair question? Would she ask it of a grown person? But I decided to be truthful. It's a marvel how many opportunities there are for dancing around the truth. "No, ma'am."

"I can give you a student card," she said, after looking me over good. "You'll be going to Jackson High, I expect. In the fall."

"Oh yes, ma'am," I said. High school was about as far away from me that day as the planet Mars. It wasn't that I hadn't planned on finishing my education. It was just that my future kept getting in the way of it.

I signed my card and tucked it away, along with my temporary Texas driver's license, expired. Bobby James said I wouldn't be needing to drive a whole lot, now that I was a wife. Which goes to show how much Bobby James knew about marital affairs. One day, in the not too far future, I was going to cruise a brand-new Chevrolet right through the streets of downtown Purley, past Woolworth's, Little Audrey's, and Purley Muffler—where Daddy worked when he did—waving at everybody in sight. I could just see Bobby James's mouth flopping open like a fish on dry land.

I started missing Purley then, in the worst way. Little things kept popping into mind as I tried to keep it busy in the pursuit of a good book. Jody + Bobby James scratched deep into the cement on the corner of Bowie and Main, there for all eternity. Sleep-overs with Kintha and Joleen where we laughed until we peed our pants. Or the best day of my whole life, when I won eighth-grade Miss Congeniality and even had a crown.

A person's whole history is no more than one little thing stacked on top of another, when you think about it.

That was when I looked down at my ten karat gold-plated wedding ring and, with the teensiest twitch in the cellar of my heart, slipped it off my finger. There was more to my history than just the good things. There was Bobby James and there was Daddy, two of a kind. There was Mama with her broken teeth and a jacked-up single-wide with four girls to a bedroom. There were Mama's hyacinths over the sink that never would grow.

Here I was all this time staring at a book on the Jackson Beach Ladies' Book Club list: The Great Gatsby. I checked it out, my first legal checkout, and took it outside to read.

Well. Misery of another kind altogether, and a lesson right when I needed one. Here was this perfectly nice person in love with somebody who never did love him and never would, a spoiled-brat rich girl named Daisy. For never letting go of the past, Mr. Jay Gatsby ended up face-down in a swimming pool. Word to the wise.

I closed the cover, filled with questions about life and what all it means, which is when you know you have got a hold of a good book.

The library lady looked surprised when I turned it back so soon. "Not your cup of tea?" she said, and I could tell what she was thinking all right, that I was not up to the caliber of a book club book.

Well, I showed *her*.

"That green light?" I said.

Her eyes sharpened right up. "The green light at the end?"

Well, it was just as I had guessed. She had read every book in that whole library.

I acknowledged that was the light all right, and so she launched right into this big lecture that left me standing high and dry on the dock just like Jay, without a clue.

"If you like Fitzgerald, you might be ready for Henry James," she said when the lecture was over. But that name was a little too close to home for me, so I told her I'd be back another day when I could browse. It was time for me to get to work, I said, stressing the work. She wasn't the only one with gainfilled employment, but I didn't say that part.

On my way to Thelma's Open 24-Hour Café and Grill, I walked past the Sandyland Apartments. There, laid out on a lounge chair, her big bare belly shining with oil, was Effaline. Toilet paper was stuck between all her toes like she had just done herself a pedicure.

Well, one thing was for sure. The Sandyland Apartments, in need of a paint job bad, wasn't much to write home about. Still, it made you wonder how a girl who got fired more than once got to live where there was an actual pool. If she could afford the place, well, maybe so could I.

I combed my hair and headed for the office with the

smeared-over window. Inside was nothing but a plaid couch with a big rip on the arm. The sunburst clock hanging on the wall said I had twenty minutes to get to work. I punched the little bell.

A bony man came out in vest underwear, scratching at his chest hairs. "Yeah?"

"I am here to inquire about the vacancy," I said, wishing I'd left my wedding ring on a little while longer.

"Fifty-five a week. One ninety-five by the month. No pets. You got kids?"

His breath was enough to knock a person out.

When I told him I was a single person, his eyes narrowed some, then went straight to my chest, which is not my most outstanding feature.

He reached for a Peg-Board full of keys and pulled one down. "This here's number 12, next to the last one down on the bottom. Bring the key right back."

By the way her hand dragged onto the cement, I could tell that Effaline was sawing logs. Her toenails were the exact color of a purple Tootsie Pop.

Well, the best you could say about number 12 was what my daddy said when Bertha Hansen came waltzing down the aisle at her third wedding wearing the same old dress: "She could use some sprucing up." I pulled open the plastic-coated drapes and the dust came off in a cloud. Then I saw why the drapes were closed in the first place. Right in the middle of the carpet was a dark brown stain in the exact shape of a human body.

I turned tail and ran right out of there.

"Well?" said the manager, in need of a sprucing himself and a good dandruff shampoo.

"If you don't mind my asking, did somebody get killed in there? Like a little while ago?"

His laugh was like a dog trying to bark with its chain pulled. "You want it or not? It's the last one I got."

Which wasn't the truth, as number 11 had the curtains open and not a stick of furniture inside.

"How about number 11?"

"That's a good deal more," he said. "You want number 12?"

"I'm still perusing the possibilities," said I, with a little chin lift. "I will let you know."

"I could let you wait some on the deposit," he said.

"I'll let you know," I said.

As I turned to leave, I tried not to think about where his eyes were. You always know with a type like that.

*M*iss Thelma was in a huff. She had just finished counting out the register, and five dollars was missing. "Not five dollars and sixteen cents, mind you, but eggzactly five dollars!"

Why sixteen cents was such a big deal, I had not one clue. So Marilyn explained that if the register was off, it would not be an even number, as thieves do not think so logical when stealing. Somebody, according to Miss Thelma, had stole that fiver, sometime between yesterday and today. Miss Thelma's beady little eyes fixed right on me.

I thank my stars that I did not choose a life of crime, as my face has been my undoing upon many an occasion. All it took were those beady eyes to break me right into a sweat.

Miss Thelma came thumping around the register and pointed her hairy nostrils straight up at me. For a shrimpy person, she was tough. I figured the FBI could have used her in that room with no windows. "Fess up, girl," she said. "The register never lies."

"No, ma'am," I said, and was about to make my case

when a portly, tall fella came swinging out from the kitchen.

"Hold on, Mama!" he said in a pipsqueak voice that didn't match at all. "That register's off all the time. Howdy," he said, sticking out his hand for a shake. "Bertram Bussard. Call me Bertie." He made the *a* in *Bussard* stick right out, making it an altogether better name.

"Jody's from Texas, Bertie," Marilyn said. "This is her third day. And she's real good, isn't she, Miss Thelma?"

Miss Thelma had been pulled down a peg by her son, who was like a good stiff breeze on a parched summer's day. She went scuttling off, muttering to herself.

Marilyn asked Bertie if he'd found a balloon, by which she meant did he buy one.

Bertie brought his squeaky voice down a notch. "Well, we don't want the word to get out just yet," he said with a glance over to the register, where Miss Thelma was busy dropping ashes on the counter. "But I'll tell you, she's the prettiest little ship you ever saw. She's got a red-and-yellow canopy without a scratch, and her gondola . . . ? Well, wait till you see." His eyes glazed over like love was in the air.

Gondola? My ears perked right up. Italy was my country in the fifth grade. It's about the most romantic place a person can go. Sometimes I still dreamed about riding a gondola down a Venice canal.

"Bertie says he's going to take us all up," Marilyn said. "But I told him over this dead and gone body!"

"I'll go!" I said, before my brain knew what my mouth was up to.

"Okay!" said Bertie, high-fiving me. "You're on! But first I've got to get some practice in. Log some time."

Having a log on a balloon didn't sound right to me. And didn't *practice* mean he didn't know how to fly the thing? Jody, I said to myself, you have got to muzzle that mouth before it gets you into some serious trouble.

"It's a pleasure to meet you, Bertie," I said, "but I got to get to work now." I figured if I stayed out of his way for a while, he'd forget what I'd said about riding in his balloon.

"That's what I like to see," Bertie said, loud enough for Miss Thelma to hear. "An employee who takes her job seriously."

Effaline comes in same as before, which is my quitting time, except that it isn't raining. She looks a good deal better dry, even with the sunburn and the stringy hair. She looks like the Before in the makeover stories.

"Hey, girlie!" she says, and the hair jumps up on my neck like a dog with the rabies. "Only kidding!" she says. "I just hate that, don't you? Come here a minute. See what I got."

For curiosity's sake I go over to the table.

Effaline reaches around her belly into her armpit. Out comes the scraggliest little cat you ever did see. "Found her sleeping in a Slurpee cup," she says. "Right out in the middle of the road. She woulda got crunched if it wasn't for me. Isn't that right, kitty? Isn't that right, sweet baby?" She dangles the kitten in front of her face and kisses its tummy.

I sit down to take the load off my feet.

In case you think it's easy work washing dishes, you should think again.

I study the cat, hanging from Effaline's hands limp as a rag doll. She looks pretty young to be on her own.

"She needs a name," says Effaline. Then, without giving it hardly a thought, she says, "Thelma. Her name's Thelma. Hi, Thelma!" She rubs noses with the little cat, who by the looks of her doesn't know what to make of anything.

"Thelma? Why name her Thelma?"

"That's where I found her. Right in front of Thelma's Café. So that's her name."

Truth is, I didn't care one way or another. In Purley we had cats like some people have rats, living all over the place. If you wanted a real pet, you got a dog, a good hunting dog, and then you put it to work. That little gray critter got to you, though. She was a long way from home, wherever that was, and had to depend entirely on the kindness of Effaline.

I tell Effaline how I stopped at her place that afternoon to inquire about the vacancy. "You were sleeping out by the pool with your toes done up."

All the smile slides right off Effaline's face like a sunnyside egg off a pan. "You don't want to live there," she says. She opens up a Half N Half. Thelma makes a dive for it, spilling it all over the table. She laps it clean in no time flat. "Kirby's a scuzzball."

In case you don't know it, scuzzball's the same in any language. "That creep comes on to you?"

"You could say that."

I thought about how, if you were a girl, you had to learn early how to swat down people like Kirby.

"But it's cheap, right?"

"Huh?"

"The rent."

"Yeah?" Like she doesn't know. She gets this far-off look in her eyes, petting the little cat as if she's half forgot it's there.

"How far are you along?"

"Pretty near the whole way." She sighs, stretching her back against her hands. "I hope Andy gets here for the birth." She says this to the window, not to me.

"Your husband?"

"Boyfriend," she says. "He's in the army. He's an admiral." Something struck me wrong about this, but I didn't know what it was. Was Effaline lying? Why would she lie? What difference did it make what a perfect stranger thought about that hickey on your neck that you got somehow, even if your boyfriend was gone?

But it did matter. You had to put a good face on things. You had to build your self of steam however you could. Effaline with her big belly and me with no home, we were not so different.

"He holds out number 11 like it's a showplace or something," Effaline says, as if we never left off on Kirby, "just because it's got the good carpet. Tell him you want number 11 and you'll pay by the week. People move in and out of that rattrap every day. Half the time without paying. He'll give it to you, don't worry. And don't go for that first and last month's crap neither."

"I need a little more time to save," I say. "I hope he doesn't rent it before I can get there."

"Don't worry. You're the first person to come by who doesn't look like the witness protection program. It'll be there."

I look at Effaline's perfect fingernails compared to mine. Even with the rubber gloves, my hands are a sight. She didn't paint them purple like her toes, just a nice soft pink, real professional. I thought about her lying in the sun while I was doing all those dishes. "What number are you in?"

"Me? Oh, I'm in the back. When you come? Don't make it too early. Kirby's a bear when he first wakes up."

She gets to her feet real careful, so as not to wake the kitten curled up on her shoulder. With her stringy hair down over it, you could hardly tell it was there. "See you tomorrow," she says. Like we're actual friends.

What fate can deal you sometimes is the Wonder of Wonders. On that peaceful July night neither Effaline nor myself had any idea of what was in store for us as we turned, her one way and me the other, and went our separate ways.

I'd about had my fill of Misery. Putting off the sneaking in till later, I passed up the cineplex and headed for the lake. The moon was like a flashlight in a black sky, lighting my way. On the bench where I had done some good hard thinking, a couple of kids were nuzzling each other. I stood behind, watching for a while, knowing I shouldn't be. The boy was tall and strong-looking like Bobby James, and the girl had a slight build with the same kind of hair as me. Right then, the night of our very first kiss, which was also Patsy Cline Night—well, it was as clear and fresh to me as a movie.

I blinked to make it disappear, along with the tears that had started up.

I parked myself on a bench farther down and tried to steer my mind to the practical things, like if I could afford a P.O. box and be saving for a place all at the same time.

Of course, if I had a place, I wouldn't need a P.O. box, so there was lots to figure out.

In my letter I had told Mama she could write to me care of Thelma's Open 24-Hour Café and Grill, hoping somebody besides Miss Thelma picked up the mail. She was the type to hold back letters just for spite.

How I was missing my mama! It wasn't easy knowing what to do when you were living in the world single. Right up to my wedding day, I had asked Mama for advice and she had given it freely. Trouble is, she couldn't take it herself. Whenever Daddy would come back and move in again? Well, she'd always make some excuse. She'd say, "This time, he won't . . ." or "This time, it's gonna be better." But of course it never was, and after a while she wasn't even trying very hard to put him off.

If you have ever looked into the eyes of a hound that's

had too many whippings, then you know how it is to look at Mama. At first the dog acts surprised, like how can you do this to me? After a while, the light fades right out of its eyes, and it waits to take whatever comes, as if it's supposed to. Like it was born to live a low-down life.

That's the thing. Somewhere along the way, all the fight went out of Mama. She got confused about the way things really were. She'd start making Daddy right. If I hadn'ta done this, he wouldn'ta done that kind of stuff.

Daddy had always stood so straight and tall, proud of all he was, even when there was no good reason. Mama had always been plain. "How I got your father to look at me, I will never know!" Mama would say, laughing through the hand she always hid her busted teeth with. For a little while, her hazel eyes would sparkle with the memory of better times. She was afraid to leave him, is the truth. By the time Daddy got through with her, she had no self of steam at all.

Sometimes I thought I was stronger than my mama, that I would never let a man like Daddy knock the fight out of me. Other times, I was not so sure. If I was back in Purley? And Bobby James came courting like he wasn't already a married man, with all those sweet promises and smelling like fresh aftershave? Well, I just didn't know for sure if I could turn him away. That was the shamefilled truth of it. Before I went back to Purley, I was going to have to find the strength in me. I didn't know exactly where to find it, or if I would know when I had it, but one thing was for sure. Letting go of Bobby James was for a reason. That morning in the Econo, I had listened to a voice deep inside me that I knew was the truth. It was only small then. It had been hiding behind Willie Nelson's words, whispering for me to stay put in the ladies'. I figured when that voice got big enough to yell in my ear, well, that was when I would have all my strength.

Sitting on that park bench in Jackson Beach, Florida, far from my Texas home, I wondered how long that would be.

*N*ext morning in the cineplex, same thing. Same funny moon face hanging down over me saying I have to wake up. No way could I beat that fella out of bed. Hard to tell what time it is, since time in a cineplex always looks the same, but I guess about 6:00 a.m. in the morning.

"Do you have a house?" he says, suspiciouslike, his chubby hands stuck on his hips. His pants are riding high-water style, like the creek's bound to rise at any time.

"Sure, I got a house."

"Oh, yeah? Well, how come you got them rollers in your hair then, huh? How come?"

I can see he has a point. I ask him what his name is, stalling for time.

He tells me it's Dooley.

"Well, Dooley," says I, "let me tell you something."

He plunks right down in a seat in front of me like it's story time.

"I'm what you call *between* houses. Know what I mean?"

He shakes his head back and forth, real slow.

"Well, it's kind of hard to explain." I reach up and pull a

pin out of a roller. Least I can do is get myself together before heading back into the world at large.

"I can do that!" Dooley says, jumping up out of his seat.
"Let me do it!" He makes a grab for my head with his short
arms, and all I can do is stay real still, holding my breath.
"Dot lets me do it at the Cut 'n' Curl. I can do it."

Tender as a mother bird, Dooley plucks out a roller and
drops it into my lap.

I let out my breath. "This is right nice of you, Dooley."

"Dot lets me do it at the Cut 'n' Curl," he says all over
again.

I pick some sleep out of my eyes. "You get up pretty
early, huh?"

"I got to make my bed," he says. "Then I can line up."

"Line up?"

"You can't be first every time," he says.

"Nope, I guess you can't."

We go on like that for a little while, getting to know
each other, more or less.

"There," Dooley says. "All done." The last roller drops
into my lap.

I almost whip out my comb, but I figure he'll make a
grab for that, too. "I'd like to use the facilities before I go.
Is that all right with you?"

"I guess it's okay," he says, but I can see that I've worried
him some. He's fingering the key he wears around his neck
real nervous. "Don't touch the candy," he says. "You're not
allowed to touch things. Only the cleaning stuff."

In the ladies' I do what I have to do, and when I come out there's Dooley, waiting. "Where'ya going now?"

You know how people forget how to be curious about stuff? It's what being grownup means, I guess. Well, Dooley's like a big little boy, filled to the top with questions that spill all over the place, like a sack of loose marbles.

I tell him that I'm going to work in a little while.

"But where'ya going now?"

Dooley follows me straight out the door and into the sunshiny day. What's my name? How old am I? Where do I go to school? Did I always remember to tell the duty girl when I come in and sign my name on the clipboard?

"There's a Ferris wheel," he says.

What does a person say to that? But that's the way Dooley talks, like there's all these things on his mind you probably didn't think of and he's just got to say them right on the spot.

"Dooley," I say, "I am a hungry working woman in bad need of a Bojangles' sausage biscuit."

Dooley looks at me with his mouth hanging open, like I am the seventeenth wonder of the world.

"Dooley? Is there a McDonald's anywhere around here?"

"Yeah! Yeah!" he says, jerking my arm about out of the socket so he can pull me the three blocks it takes to get there.

He watches me eat my number 3 bacon-and-egg biscuit with orange juice and coffee without saying so much as a word, never taking his eyes off my mouth. Every now and then, he heaves this big heavy sigh and shifts around a little in his seat. It's a thing that makes a person extra careful with their manners, but doesn't help the food settle, if you know what I mean.

I chew my last bite and crumple up the wrap.

"Is it time for the Ferris wheel now?" He looks at me like I am special, and I can't think how to say no.

In no time at all I am riding the Ferris wheel like a person of leisure. Lucky for me, the operator knows Dooley and lets him ride for free. Me, too, but that is only to look up my skirt. After it's tucked under real good, he quits looking.

Dooley walks me all the way to Thelma's. I figure he's going to follow me straight into the kitchen, so I tell him it's time for me to get to work.

He stands there, waiting for I don't know what. "It's okay if you sleep in a seat," he says. "I won't tell."

"Thank you, Dooley. I appreciate that."

"I'll wake you up so you can go to work."

"Okay," I say. "See you later." The door closes behind me, then it snaps back open.

"Jody!" He shrieks like his hand got caught in the door.

"What's the matter, Dooley?"

"I forgot to sweep!"

"Oh." I didn't know what to say. He looks like he's just murdered somebody and doesn't know where to hide the body.

"I forgot to sweep! I'm gonna get in trouble."

He was going to wring those hands right off if I didn't say something fast.

"When's the first show? When's it start, Dooley?"

"One-twenty, three-thirty, five-forty, seven fifty-five," says Dooley, like he's doing his multiplication tables.

I tell him it's okay. "It's only ten till eleven. You still got plenty of time to sweep."

He thinks hard about that for a minute, then he hurries off without a goodbye, still wringing those hands.

All this time Marilyn's been watching without watching, if you know what I mean.

My eyes follow Dooley through the window as he hurries toward the cineplex. "Poor guy, I hope he doesn't lose his job."

"Dooley?" Marilyn says with a laugh. "He doesn't have a real job, not one he gets paid for anyway. People just let him do odd jobs and such. Mostly the heavy stuff. He's strong as an ox."

Marilyn said Dooley lived in a group home, and so I finally understood about the signing in on the clipboard and the lining up. "I never could understand how a parent could give up such a sweet kid . . ."

"You mean he's never had parents?"

"Nope. His mother, if you could call her that, threw him out the day he was born."

"You mean—?"

"Yeah. In the Dumpster behind the Walgreens."

"Some people," I said, fuming, seeing that sweet little moon face among the rotten tomatoes.

"Yeah. Some people!" Marilyn shook her head sadly.

"Kids used to call him Dooley Dumpster or Dooley Drooley. So he stopped going to school. Kids can be so mean."

Well, there wasn't much to be done about something that was already done, except a lot of clucking tongues and shaking heads. I headed for the kitchen. Marilyn went back to marrying the catsups, which means dumping the one into the other, according to her. Even though there were only three people in the whole place, I knew the dishes would be piled up from the night before, like always. But it was something to count on, in a funny kind of way, like I had a reason to be that I didn't have before. When there's nothing else to be done about a thing, my mama always said, you can always clean up a mess.

The days went by like they do. On one of them I showed up for work early and there was Bertie giving Enrique a cooking lesson at the prep table. Enrique, being a breakfast cook of Latin origin, didn't have much experience with chopping cabbage, and Bertie was showing him the right way, which is to hold on to that cabbage with your fingers all curled under. Then the knife can slide right close without chopping anything but what you want it to.

It's an artful thing done right.

I'd been meaning to say something about the coleslaw and took this for the time. But I stood there biting my tongue just the same, coleslaw being, as everybody knows, not the dishwasher's job.

We said our hi's. I watched until the cabbage was in the

big bowl and Bertie was about to slop all that mayonnaise in.

"You really oughtn'ta do it that way," I said. It slipped right out, as my feelings about coleslaw are a good deal stronger than I had thought.

Bertie's hand with the big spoon stopped short of the bowl. He looked over at me with his eyebrows halfway up his baldy head, and I thought, Uh-oh. "I guess you Texans got the best recipe for coleslaw, right? Just like you got the best everything else." He shook his head, but he was smiling at the same time. Then he slopped the mayo in.

Well, I just wanted to slap his hand. But of course I couldn't, I could hardly think it, him being my boss and all. I just stood there thinking, it was no wonder the dishes came back full of food. A slop of coleslaw on a person's plate is a dead giveaway of a low-class eating establishment if ever there was one.

Marilyn poked her head through the door. "Here's a letter for you, Jody."

"For me?" She handed it over.

What to my wondering eyes but a letter from home with only one corner of it slopped with catsup! I wanted to tear it open right then, but due to my good breeding, duty was put before love.

I folded Mama's letter and tucked it into the back pocket of my jeans. I would read it on my break, which is a law I didn't know a thing about until Bertie informed me of it. Fifteen minutes all my own every three hours. I fairly sailed through those dishes, Mama's letter lighting the way before me like a beacon of hope.

But the news was not good. Opening Mama's envelope carefully with a butter knife, sliding out the folded page, I smoothed it on the table and began to read.

Dearest daughter,

I hope this letter finds you well, as you are a source of great surprise to your family ever since the day you took your first baby steps off the back porch. Pastor says your place is with your husband, Bobby James Walker, and you will come to your senses, but I said that I did not know about that, senses being what we Hoopers have not got in great store. I figured I told you about all I could before you went off but one thing, which is a man is not going to wait, if you know what I mean. If his wife is not right there where and when he wants her, well, he will be looking around, you can count right on that. I don't know why Bobby James left you behind, but all I'm saying is it's not too late to make it up. Word to the wise. Well, to change the subject. Daddy is working some with the mufflers and getting there on time most every day, which is the good news. Be a good girl and stay out of trouble and come home soon.

Your loving mother

Well, I read that letter over three times, dripping tears until I had used half a dispenser of napkins. Daddy was home again. How else would Mama know what time he was getting to work? And what would he do with his paycheck on Friday but cash it at Harley's Cash and Carry, straight across from the Watering Hole bar.

I knew what would come after that, too.

I went back to the kitchen, this heart in a sorry slump.

"You okay, *chica*?" Enrique caught me with his sad dark eyes.

"Yes, thank you." I put on my rubber gloves and watched the greasy gray water swirl down the drain.

"The coleslaw?" Enrique had come over and was standing by the sink. We were at eye level, which means that Enrique is short for a man, which means nothing when you get right down to it, my daddy being tall but small.

"*Mañana*? You make the coleslaw. You will feel better, no?"

Well, if that wasn't the sweetest thing. But of course I told him how we'd both get in trouble, as coleslaw making was not the dishwasher's job.

"*Mañana*? Señor Boosardo's day off. You make the coleslaw." He crossed his arms as if that was that.

Quitting time and, sure as ticks on a hound, there's Effaline and Thelma the cat. Effaline has filled an ashtray with about twenty Half N Half, and Thelma is making short work of it.

"I told Kirby you were interested in number 11," Effaline says.

"And . . . ?"

"Well, you know Kirby." As if I did. "He says number 11 is not available and blah blah blah. So I say, Well then, she's going to take one of those town houses over on Johnson Avenue that they just did a makeover on, complete with built-ins and a dishwasher."

"And . . ."

It took Effaline a little while to get to the main point sometimes.

She shrugs. "Number 11 is yours, if you want it. But like I said, you gotta watch old Kirby. Doesn't she, Thelma, honey, baby, sweet girl?" She lifts Thelma and her little legs go limp. She just hangs there waiting for Effaline to get over all that loving on her.

I'm busy figuring out my money, which does not take me long. "Are you sure he'll wait for the deposit?"

"Oh, yeah. Like I said, he can't keep the place full. He pockets those deposits anyway, like they're his personal bonus or something. Then just try to get it back!" She laughs, shaking her head. "He's a piece of work, all right."

There's a knock on the window. It's Dooley.

We both wave at him, which is how I can tell Effaline knows him, too. Dooley comes in and I scoot over so he can sit. Well, he gets right to work on that poor cat, petting it until I thought its fur would wear off. "When are you coming to the show, Jody?"

Well, the truth will out, as Mama always says. One thing leads to another and pretty soon my whole story is laid out like a table at a flea market.

"That's where you're staying? The cineplex?" Effaline's eyes just about pop out of her head.

"No!" Dooley yells. "She's got a house. Right, Jody? Right, Jody?"

So I tell him again what I told him before about being between houses, which doesn't fool old Effaline for a minute.

"Well, if that don't beat all," she says. "I never thought about that, about, like, living in a movie theater. But I suppose you could, I mean if you are . . ."

"Jody's not living there," says Dooley, but he's looking pretty confused. "Jody's between houses. Right, Jody? You're between houses."

"Yeah," says Effaline, rolling her eyes. "Like I'm between jobs!"

"Right, Dooley, between houses," says I, but I'm feeling pretty low. You can make a thing out of what you will, but it won't always hold a shine when a good hard light is thrown upon it.

Word to the wise.

"Jody's got a new place now, Dooley," says Effaline. "Number 11 Sandyland Apartments. She's gonna be my new neighbor."

And that's when Effaline smiles for the first real time.

*E*ffaline was right. Kirby gives me no more trouble than a snake eyeing the digging end of a shovel. He grabs my first week's rent out of my hand and shoves me the key to number 11. When I ask for a written receipt, he acts real put-upon, but he fills out the record book after some whining about it, biting on his tongue the whole time to write.

"Be sweet and I'll see to it you get your phone hooked up by Friday," he says.

"I'm done with sweet," says I. "I'm on to sour now. It gets a whole lot more done, if you know what I mean."

And you know what? I think he did.

Effaline is waiting at the door to number 11. Instead of Thelma, what she has in her skinny arms is a lamp with a frilly skirt hanging down over a buffalo. "Figured you'd need this," she says.

I take a deep breath and open the door to my very own first apartment. The stale smell makes me run to open up every window in the place, three total, plus the little bitty one in the bathroom. Effaline plugs in the lamp and sets it on the floor. Then she opens the refrigerator, the oven, the medicine chest, and the closet, poking her head into all of them.

I ask her, isn't it just like hers?

"Mine? Oh, my apartment? Yeah, more or less. But like I said, you got the best carpet." She plunks down and crosses her legs Indian-style, cradling her belly in there like a beach ball. Then she runs her hand over it all dreamylike, as if she's listening to something only she can hear. "We got to get you some furniture," she says. "I can loan you a blanket and a pillow for starters." She sticks out her hand. "Help me up," she says and wanders off.

I put my possessions in their rightful places. My curlers go into the one little drawer in the bathroom, along with my toothbrush, toothpaste, shampoo, and comb. Then I put my comb back into my bag, seeing as I have only the one. My clothes I stack neatly on the shelf in the closet.

And that is that. I am home.

It's kind of funny, though. Never have I felt farther from home in my life. When I was that little kid running away? This was the time I'd turn around and head back.

I shut the almost empty closet with a lump in my throat.

I am writing Mama with my new address when Effaline comes back. She is hauling a pool raft, a blanket, Thelma, and a cat box. "Can she stay with you awhile?"

Well, Thelma doesn't look like she cares a whole lot where she stays, as long as it's warm and dry. As soon as Effaline sets her box down, she gets right to using it.

I figure I owe Effaline. "Uh, sure, she can stay awhile. But why? I mean, why here?"

Thelma's scratching her way through that litter straight down to China.

"Kirby won't let me keep her. He hates cats."

I think about that some. "Well, he's not going to let me keep her either then, right?"

She swishes her hands like she's washing a window. "Oh no. It's okay. It's not like there's a rule or anything."

Something's all wrong about this. I am missing a stitch somewhere and don't know where to look for it.

Well, it gets to be supper time and there Effaline still is. As I do not have a single plate to put food on, or the food in the first place, I am not in a position to offer supper to my guest.

I ask Effaline if she would like some barbecue, my treat.

She springs right up like a skinny girl. "I'd give my life for a pulled-pork sandwich," she says.

The sun is in a meltdown as we cross the highway to Sonny's. It made you wonder, like I always did, why all the best sunsets happen in the strip malls. But as Mama always says, God works His mysterious ways.

"My daddy made the best barbecue," Effaline says when we are sitting in our booth. "Secret recipe." She takes a honking bite of her sandwich, juice running all down her chin. What she says next I can't make out, as her mouth is full.

In case you're wondering, Sonny's coleslaw is better than you would expect, what with the decor.

I didn't know much about Effaline's life then. She was from "around here," she had told me once, and I let it go at that. But I was curious, like you always are about folks. "You keep in touch with your mama and daddy, Effaline?"

Some folks leap right into the good stuff without an eye blink. Others hang back and make you ask. Effaline is a hang-backer. "My mom," she says. "Sometimes."

"I guess she'll be here for the birth, huh?"

Effaline shrugs. "Probably not."

Wild horses could not keep my mama from a grandchild's birth, I can tell you that. Any birth at all, for that matter. I have to ask Effaline why.

Her sandwich is history. She wipes off her face and hands, frowning the whole time. "Jody? My mother doesn't believe one thing I say."

"Nothing?"

"Not when it counts."

And that's when she tells me the story of her stepfather, which does not bear repeating in polite company.

"I took off when I was fourteen," she says, when she's finished the telling. "Been on my own ever since. Almost a year and a half."

"You're only fifteen?"

"Yeah. Why?"

I shrug. "I don't know. You look older."

Her face lights up like I've made her day. "I do?"

With her eyes done right she'd be a real pretty girl, is what I'm thinking. "Yeah."

"Well, I was always mature for my age," she says, flipping back her hair.

Well, I didn't know about that.

But fair's fair. I tell her about Bobby James and me. About Patsy Cline Night and the wedding, our life in the Duster, and then the shrimp and coleslaw.

She lets out this huge belch that turns everybody around in their seats. "That the first time he belted you?"

"First time." After all that had happened to Effaline, it was hard not to shrink that slap right down to nothing.

Then I remember how it felt.

She shrugs. "He probably just loved you too much."

"Effaline, that does not make one bit of good sense."

"Love doesn't always make sense," Effaline says, like she's read it in some romance book.

We walk back to Sandyland in one of those quiet places where you stack your life up against the one whose shoes you wouldn't want to walk a mile in.

When Effaline's back at her place, I make me a bed with the pool raft next to the buffalo lamp. I sleep pretty good, too, except when I have to blow up that leaky raft. Thelma doesn't mind. She just settles back down on my head without missing one purr.

At Thelma's Open 24-Hour Café and Grill, Enrique's got the cabbage and the big bowl all laid out. When he sees me, he steps aside and bows real formal, laying the knife over his hand like Zorro's sword.

I make short work of that cabbage, chopping it into fine shreds but not so fine as to wimp it out when the dressing gets in. Then I set about mixing in all the ingredients. I dig out a forkful and offer it to Enrique, who kisses his fingers like an Italian, which he is not, but some things do translate.

I hand Enrique the spoon just in time, because in comes Miss Thelma.

"What's all this lollygaggin'?" she says. "Ain't you got dishes to do, girlie?"

"Yes, ma'am," I say.

"You got your scrubber?"

"Yes, ma'am."

"You make sure that water is hot, hear?"

"Yes, *ma'am!*"

She turns on her cane to leave.

"Miss Thelma?" I say, all sweetly.

"Yeah?" She works and works her mouth, even when there's not a thing in it but her tongue.

"Do you like coleslaw?"

She narrows those beady little eyes like Snow White's wicked stepmother. I guess she figures I'll poison her, first chance I get. "Why?"

I cross my fingers behind my back. "Oh, no reason, except I had some of it, uh, *yesterday*. It's the best coleslaw I have ever tasted. Counting my own mama's, which is an old family recipe."

"Well." She works that tongue until she can get the words out. "Slaw gives me gas."

"Not this kind. Maybe you'll want to try some with your lunch," I say, spinning on the hot water tap full blast.

This is how to get one good free facial, in case you're wondering.

"Maybe I will," says Miss Thelma. "And maybe I won't."

"And maybe you won't," I say, like a mockingbird.

But she's got the ears of a good bird dog. "What's that, girlie?"

"Not a blessed thing, Miss Thelma."

Little puffs of air are popping out of Enrique like a pressure cooker. If she doesn't leave quick, he's going to explode, which he does the minute she's gone. We have a good laugh then, both of us wiping our eyes on fresh clean towels from the linen supply.

I learn two songs: "Vaya con Dios" and "Cielito Lindo," both in the Spanish language, and the hours pass like that.

I take my break at two, just as Marilyn is starting her

shift. I tell her all about my new apartment. Lo and behold, what has she got but a bunch of stored furniture ready for the taking.

"It's not antiques or nothing. Just stuff I had from, you know, when I was married last and, well, the time before that. Couldn't fit it all into my studio, so I got it in storage. You're welcome to whatever you need."

I tell her I can't pay her yet but I will.

"It's a loan, darlin'," she says. "Until you get stuff you like. Your own kind of stuff."

She tells me to come by the next morning, not too early.

Bertie slides into the booth smelling of Old Spice. "What're you gals cooking up?"

Bertie's sweet on Marilyn, anybody can see how bad.

"Are you busy in the morning?" Marilyn asks him. You can see she knows it, too.

Bertie looks like he's won the Powerball. "I'm not doing a thing. What do you need?"

"It's Jody here," she says. "She could use some help moving furniture into her new place."

His face drops down a little, but good person that he is, he offers to meet me at Marilyn's at ten.

"Enrique really got the hang of that coleslaw," says Bertie, sliding out of the booth. "Try some, Jody. If it don't beat that Texas stuff, I'll buy you a steak dinner."

"I believe I will."

I make a dash for the kitchen before busting up.

When Effaline comes in at the end of my shift, I tell her all about my good fortune. She's almost as excited as me. "I hope there's twin beds," she says. Then she sits there with her mouth stuck open. "I mean, you know, in case somebody wants to stay over or something." She shrugs.

The next morning at Marilyn's is just like *The Price Is Right*. Marilyn opens up her storage and there, stacked every which way, is about every kind of furniture a person could think up. I pick out a couch with orange and yellow zigzags, a chair to match, a Formica table with hardly one scratch, and four red chairs. Marilyn loads in a coffee table with a genuine marble top and two boodwar lamps.

"There's a TV in here somewhere," she says, heading back into the storage.

"You'll need a bed," Bertie says, tilting down a mattress.

"There's a matching set," Marilyn says, carrying out a pink TV with rabbit ears. "Do you want the other bed, too?"

I think about it a little longer than a good person would. I try not to worry about Effaline, but it's hard not to. She had gotten herself smack into the middle of my life without my hardly knowing. "Sure. If it's a set, I guess I should keep it together."

Bertie's pickup is piled over the top. We drive off, waving to Marilyn until she's just this little bitty thing in the mirror.

I babble on for a while about what a great person Marilyn is, which Bertie already knows.

"Can you keep a secret?" he says, turning left onto Sandyland Avenue.

I pull out my key, which is tied on a ribbon and attached to the strap of my drawstring bag for safekeeping. "It all depends."

"On what?" says Bertie, all surprised. Why people expect you to keep their secrets for them without a second thought is more than I can understand.

"On whether it's gonna hurt somebody or not."

"I wouldn't hurt her for the world," he says, sticking his hand straight over his heart.

"Marilyn?"

"I'm going to ask her to marry me," he says. "Guess where?"

It doesn't take a genius to figure it out. "In the balloon?"

"Bingo!"

Well, according to Marilyn, she was "never, ever going to get married in this life again, so help me God." You have got to take a three-time loser pretty serious. But Bertie's face is glowing like he's already seeing her dressed all in white, veil drifting behind that red-and-yellow balloon as it sails through the clouds.

"But she said she was never—" I gulp and shut my fat mouth.

His eyes are big as beach balls. "What?"

"Uh, never going up in that balloon! Over her dead and gone body, she said."

"Oh!" Bertie laughs. "Everybody says that. Then they watch a balloon going up and they can't wait to jump on. You'll see."

And so there I am worrying all over again. "You been getting the logs and all?"

"Logs?"

"Yeah, the logs. Like you said."

"Logging time you mean? Sure. Every chance I get."

Which is a relief.

With Effaline's help, as much as she can do, we get the furniture all in place. Marilyn had even thrown in some matching sheets and the prettiest picture of two swans on a lake.

"They mate for life, you know," she had said, in a misty sort of way. Then she flat out snorted. "A life with any man is about two lifetimes too long, if you ask me!"

Well, it was good Bertie didn't have his mother's talent for hearing.

When Bertie's gone, I go around straightening the couch pillows, the swan picture, and the lamp shade like a proud owner. Even if I was only a proud borrower, it had the same feel about it.

"Effaline?"

Thelma's doing her thing in the box again, but Effaline is nowhere in sight. I check the bedroom and there she is, sound asleep on one of the twins. Her hands are crossed on her chest like a dead person, which gives me a start at first. But no matter what you hear to the contrary, the dead never do look that peaceful and happy to be where they are.

I close the door quietly, feeling downright sorry that we have wore her out. A woman in that time of life should not be moving furniture. If the cord wrapped itself around that baby's neck, I knew I could never forgive myself.

I leave Effaline a note saying I am going to the Hacienda Thrift for some kitchenware. I figure it wasn't a place she'd ever want to go to again anyway.

Another cashier is on duty. This one isn't in the family way and she does know how to do the register, one thing not having much to do with the other, but still it makes you think.

ALL PICTURES HALF OFF says the sale sign. I was wishing for pots and pans instead, but you had to pass the pictures to get there and it didn't hurt to look. The swans were in the bedroom over the twins, which left the couch needing something to set it off bad.

Well, the air whooshes right up out of me as soon as I see it. Venice with the big blue dome. A handsome Italian man in a red-and-white striped shirt is singing to a couple wrapped together as he pushes that gondola down the canal with his steering pole. It has $9.99 marked in black crayon across the front.

Well, 50 percent is still a lot to pay for a picture that small, but once it's in my hands, wild alligators could not have ripped it from me. I have just enough left for a cooking pot, a plate, a fork, the khaki slacks right where I left them, and a teakettle without the whistle. That is when I remember the sauce.

I look at the kettle a good long while before deciding, hamburger or tea? But what's a house without a good cup of tea? Not a home, I can tell you that.

You can always do a good spaghetti sauce without the meat. The Italians do it all the time.

*T*here I was with too much in my arms and Venice heading for a fall, when who should turn up but Dooley.

"Where ya goin', Jody?"

I loaded him down with everything but Venice.

"I am going to my new place, Dooley. Twenty-two twenty-three Sandyland Avenue, apartment number 11." I liked that number so much, I'd say it out loud in the shower. "My new home."

"Is it a between-house?" Dooley wanted to know, but we got that straightened out soon as he saw I was living in the same place as Effaline.

He followed me right in, about as excited as I was, turning the key for the very first time. He opened and closed the refrigerator a couple of times like it's a magic trick.

Then he set out to explore.

"Effaline!" Dooley hurried back out of the bedroom. "Jody! Effaline's sleeping in your bed."

"No, I'm not!" said Effaline. Out she comes, yawning and stretching.

The things that girl didn't know worried the life out of me. "You oughtn'ta raise your arms that high, you know."

"How come?"

"You can wrap the cord around your baby's neck," I told her, which any fool knows.

"Old wife's tale," she said. She turned away, muttering. "Besides, the baby won't be mine. Not for long."

Dooley's head was swiveling from one of us to the other, but I don't think he was taking much in.

"Effaline?" My voice was this quiet little mouse inside me.

"What?" she said, scratching her belly.

"Are you giving this baby up?"

A car drove by outside with Spanish music turned full blast. Upstairs a lady yelled, "Over my dead body!" Which reminded me of Marilyn, which made me think about Marilyn's daughter killed by the drunk driver, which made me think how much she would want her grownup baby back, which brought me back to Effaline.

Effaline shrugged. "What else can I do?"

Well, there was an answer to that plain as day.

"I got no job, no place to . . ." She gave me a quick glance that slid away just as quick. "No . . . money."

"What about Andy? Doesn't he send you money?"

"I got some money," Dooley said, feeling around in his pockets.

"Huh? Oh, sure, but it's not a whole lot. You know the army. Hey, what'cha got, Jody? Another picture?"

I turned Venice around for her to see, even if she was just changing the subject like she does.

"It's sort of . . . nice," she said with a little shrug, which told you a whole lot about Effaline's taste.

"Jody's making us spaghetti for dinner," said Dooley. He'd already put away the pot, fork, and plate, and set the teakettle on the stove.

"Oh, good," said Effaline, like she really didn't know where her next meal was coming from, which she probably didn't, come to think of it. "I'm starved."

So there I was with three for dinner, instead of one with leftovers for the next two nights. But spaghetti always tastes better when shared, like about everything else I can think of.

I put the water on to boil and sent Effaline back to her place for extra forks and plates.

While that was happening, I started a list on the refrigerator and stuck it with a Purley Plumbers magnet that had been rattling around in my bag.

CANDLE is what I wrote as number 1, which is not a practical item but which adds that special touch to any store-bought meal. But I don't think Dooley knew the difference between sauce from the jar and homemade, as he polished off what was left on Effaline's plate as well as his own without hardly looking up.

"I got to go have my dinner now," he said, getting up. He carried his plate and fork to the sink like a regular gentleman and rinsed them off.

"You just had your dinner," said Effaline.

"No," said Dooley. "I got to have my dinner now."

Effaline shrugged, as if to say go figure.

"There's rules, I guess," she said, when Dooley was gone.

I took a good hard look at Effaline, who was, after all, a person of very short acquaintance, and I thought about Dooley, the way he was just lying there in the tomatoes waiting for a life. Would Effaline do such a thing to her baby?

Instead of asking, which how could I do, I asked when she heard last from her boyfriend.

She heaved this big sigh. "Jody?"

"Yeah?" But I knew what she was going to say sure as I know the birthmark on my right knee in the exact shape of the state of Texas.

"There's no Andy."

"Who is there, then?"

She shook her head like a duck shaking water off its beak. The refrigerator hummed. A door slammed upstairs. From a ways off, a dog yelped like a coyote.

"You don't know or you won't say?"

Effaline flopped up out of her chair. "What's the difference?" She stuck her hands on her hips and pushed her belly straight out, almost like she's proud. "What's done is done." Her hand went to the top of her belly and her eyes got real wide. "Oooooh! That was a good one."

"It's kicking?"

"Right here, right here," she said, grabbing up my hand. She plastered it where hers had been. And what do you know but that a tiny foot or a knee pokes right into the flat of my hand.

We stood there staring at each other like we'd both seen Elvis.

I do not sleep but six or seven winks. There's the question of Effaline in the other bed for one thing, and my hand that keeps feeling that little poke for another.

She didn't even ask to stay over, is the thing. Once we finish watching the TV like regular folks, up Effaline gets from the couch. I figure she's heading for the potty, but no, she's back on the bed and fast asleep.

I lie there listening to the wind whipping around the corner of the building. There's been some talk of a hurricane, but I don't let it worry me, as anybody growing up in tornado country would probably not.

Word to the wise.

I stare up at the ceiling and wonder what Bobby James is doing right this minute. Here I am, a married lady who should be sleeping in her marriage bed, not in a twin across from a person of short acquaintance.

Effaline is on her back on top of the covers because of the heat, snoring these little snores.

BANG! BANG! BANG! "Effaline! You in there, Effaline?"

I nearly jump out of my underwear.

The door is banging off its hinges. "Effaline," says I. "Somebody's yelling for you."

"Kirby," she groans, crossing her arms over her eyes.

"What's Kirby want with you?"

BANG! BANG! Then the handle starts rattling. If it's Kirby, I figure he's got a spare key.

"Tell him to go away," she says, sitting half up.

Kirby yells for Effaline to get her skinny blank-a-blank out there.

"You tell him," says I.

He starts in serious then, like somebody who never did get their mouth washed out good enough with soap when it should have been.

She sits full up then, that same scared-rabbit look on her face. "Tell him!"

Then she sees that won't work.

"Please? Please, Jody?"

I stomp out and yell at the back of the door. "She says to go away!"

Some glass crashes to the cement. Kirby cusses. I run and grab a kitchen chair. I wedge it tight under the knob. Effaline is standing in the doorway to the bedroom holding Thelma up under her chin.

For a little while, it's quiet. Thelma yawns.

I peek out the drapes. I can't get a good look at the stoop. "If I had a phone, we could call the police."

Effaline's eyes get wide. "No! You can't do that. They got my face on a missing-kids poster!"

"You figuring on fighting off a grown man? A grown drunk man? We need the police."

"Maybe he's gone," she says.

But she's wrong.

A key rattles in the lock. I jump into the chair. Effaline flies across the room and lands in my lap.

"What the—?" Kirby pushes all his weight against the door, but he isn't enough for the both of us. Then it's quiet again. We sit listening with Thelma, who's in the middle of the room with her ears stuck straight out like Yoda. We hear barfing. Then something hits the door once, hard. We wait a long while, Effaline making my legs go numb.

After a while, I push her up off my lap. "Effaline, is that baby Kirby's?"

I stand there shaking in my underwear. It's the middle of the night, time for some hard questions any way you look at it.

"Swear to God it's not his," Effaline says, crossing her heart.

"Then . . . ?"

She shrugs.

"You don't know?"

She shakes her head, her eyes sliding away like it's more than she wants to think about at that moment, or any other time either.

She sets the chair aside and opens the door. "See you to-morrow," she says.

"Where are you going?"

She shrugs. "Kirby's."

"But why?"

She sighs like a teacher who's tried to teach you six plus

six for about a month and you just won't get it. "That's where I'm living, Jody."

"But why?"

"I already told you. I'm flat busted."

"But he's a snake, Effaline. You don't have to—"

"Thanks for dinner," she says with this weary, sad little smile, just like the ones I remembered from home.

*T*he wind starts kicking up about the time I'm heading for work. It makes me mad, as I have taken great pains with my hair. I hug myself, wishing I had brought a sweater. Well, what I'm wishing is that I owned a sweater. You wouldn't think you'd ever need one in Florida, but you do.

It doesn't look a bit like Florida right then. Not the Florida in the postcards anyway, which is what I was getting used to. The sky was an ugly gray, like a storm was brewing. I started moving faster. If a hurricane was coming, I figured I'd better be inside somewhere.

By the time I get to Miss Thelma's, I am clean out of breath.

And there's everybody sitting at a six-top like regular customers, when they ought to be working.

"Jody! What are you doing here?"

"Well, I have come to work."

I had been overoccupied with other things and could have got the schedule wrong.

"Ain't you been watching the TV?" Miss Thelma says. "You're supposed to watch the TV for hurricanes. Everybody knows that."

"It's been hanging out off the coast," Marilyn says, filing her nails. "Probably won't head this way at all."

"Here's another report," Bertie says, and we all turn to look at the set.

Well, it's a no-news-is-good-news thing. The hurricane, Emma her name is, has stalled itself.

"Sit down," Bertie says. "Take a load off."

I pull out a chair.

"The biggest storm I was ever in was in the army, up in Fort Dix," Bertie says.

Then we're all swapping storm stories. For every hurricane of theirs, I dig up a tornado twice as mean.

"Listen to the girl," Miss Thelma says. "Sounds like a tourist. I'll tell you good, girlie. If you ever get caught in the eye of a full-out hurricane, you'll shut your trap once and for all."

"You get caught in the eye of a hurricane and you're toast," Marilyn says, blowing smoke at the ceiling.

"You know what I mean," Miss Thelma snaps. "You feel that eye over top of you . . ."

We all look up at the flyspecks on the ceiling along with her.

"And everything gets so dead and still"—she flutters her skinny fingers like she's telling a ghost story—"you can't even find the air to breathe one breath. And there's no sound a'tall, nothing. It's like a trap ready to—"

"That's enough, Mother," Bertie says, wiping sweat off his forehead. "You're scaring the pants off Jody here."

But I'm not one bit scared. "One time in Purley—?"

The weather lady comes back on the screen. Emma is moving south and heading straight for us. We are on Official Hurricane Warning.

"Well, I'll be darned," Marilyn says, still filing.

"Might as well start taping the windows," Bertie says, popping up. "You all go on home. Batten down the hatches. It sounds like we're in for a good storm."

"We can help," Marilyn says. "That'll get us all out of here faster."

We keep a good eye on the sky through the windows while we tape. It's darker and lower than it was, with clouds starting to build like shaving foam. Palm trees are blowing sideways. Whole sheets of newspaper go flying past the windows.

"Okay, I think that'll do it," says Bertie. "Mother and I will take Jody home. Anybody else need a ride?"

The wind pushes against us as we head for the pickup. Bertie's got Miss Thelma's arm tucked under his so she won't fly off. They drop me at my place. "Call if you get scared," Bertie says.

I watch them drive off, them thinking I've got me a phone, which most everybody has. It's the second time in two days I've needed a thing that I do not need.

Sandyland Apartments looks like everybody's headed for the high ground, of which there is none in Florida. Not a soul anyplace, not even Kirby, and not one window taped. The beach chairs are every which way, along with branches from the palm trees. A banana peel is floating in the pool with a big old cockroach riding on top of it.

The things you see!

With the tape that Bertie was kind enough to give me, I tape my windows in six different directions before going in.

Then what's there to do but change into shorts and make me a good strong cup of tea to wait out the storm.

I get three letters done, one to Mama, one to Kintha, my best friend, and the last to Joleen, my second-best friend, before the lights go off. Each letter is a little different, which is another funny thing when you think about it. I mean, it's my same life. Mama's is the most happy sounding of the three, as I would not worry her for the world and all its gold.

Just as I'm licking the last envelope, what should happen again but the banging on the door and Kirby yelling his fool head off.

This time I get up and open the door right in his face. It's almost as dark outside as it is where I'm standing. What's left of Kirby's greasy hair is blowing south.

"She's not here," I tell him.

"What do you mean, she's not here?"

Kirby's another of your shorter men but he's strong. You can see it in the way he's wired together. Both arms have tattoos you wouldn't brag about if you were a decent person of taste.

"What I mean is that she is not here. As in *not here*. Get it?"

He sticks his jaw out. "Where is she, then?"

"Cow should I know?" That fast, he has got me down to his level.

"Figures," he says, sucking his teeth. "She's too dumb to come in out of the rain, that's for damn sure." He stomps off, muttering to himself.

"Wait! Where do you think she went?" But the wind flings my words back at me.

"Aw, Effaline," says I, looking up at that angry sky.

I know where she is, all right. She's standing at the door to Miss Thelma's, her and the cat peering into the dark of an empty café. I take a quick look behind me at all the homely comfort, and then I push out into the storm, locking the door behind me.

If I don't look for Effaline, who else is going to bother?

The wind tears at my hair like it means to do me serious harm, but I ball up and head straight into it. There's only the one good way to go, a left on Sandyland for two blocks, then a right on Central. If Effaline's heading for home, I figure I'll find her soon enough.

A couple of cars pass, the people inside scootched low like the wind could snatch them right out of their seats. Pieces of paper are plastered against the chain-link fence where a Texaco used to be. NEED A JOB? says one piece, hanging there in the wind. It makes me think how this darned Emma is keeping me from working. No way will Miss Thelma pay me for dishes that don't get done.

Thinking about all the meals I won't get to eat makes me hungry.

I turn right on Central and scoot along close to the telephone company, which saves me from the worst of the wind. No folks out but me. This is worrisome, but not near so much as seeing Thelma's Open 24-Hour Café and Grill with nobody in front of it. Over my head the palm leaves are going wild, flapping like banners at the races. Trash dances and rolls down the middle of the street. Teeny grains of sand sting my bare legs.

"Effaline!" It's like yelling in the cellar just to hear yourself yell. Nobody's there, but it makes you feel better when you hear your own voice.

I head up Central, toward Walgreens and the cineplex. There's tape on all the windows, except the stores that went out of business.

A low growl starts up behind me. I whip around, but it's only the mournful cry of the wind. I'm run-walking fast as I can, all hunched over, with my fists stuck down in the pockets of my shorts.

That's when I see something round and white huddled in the entranceway to the cineplex.

"Effaline? Effaline!"

The wind pushes me sideways across Central as if it means to clear the street of me.

It's Effaline all right. Thelma, too, all tucked into one miserable ball. I yell "Effaline!" over the screech of the wind. I grab her shoulder and start shaking it.

She looks up, her almost blue eyes lost and dizzy-looking.

They clear a little when she sees it's me. "Where were you, Jody? Where were you?"

"I'm right here, Effaline. Get up now. Come on, we gotta get home."

I lift poor Thelma out of her arms. She digs her claws into my shoulder and holds on without any help. I grab under the armpits of Effaline's man's shirt and try hoisting her, but it's a trial. "Come on, Effaline. Get up!"

I get her to her feet at last when, splat, her water breaks right there at the cineplex door.

"Oh, no!" cries Effaline. "Look! Look what I did!"

She stares at the puddle like a kid who's peed her pants in kindergarten.

For a minute I stare, too. Water means your baby's on its way, any fool knows that. But there's only me and Effaline. The baby can't come now!

A huge bolt of lightning splits the sky in half.

Effaline stands there holding up her stomach. "Jody! What do we do now? Am I gonna die?"

"It's all right, Effaline. You're not gonna die. It's just your water. Come on. We got to—"

But she crumples right back down and squats there like a chicken. "Owwwwww!" she cries. "It hurts! It hurts!"

"Is it starting? Is your labor starting, Effaline?"

"I don't know! How should I know? I never had a baby before. Ohhhh, owwww!"

I look out at the street, wild for somebody to come. Anybody! The only phone is inside Walgreens, back by the Tide, but it is shut down like everything else.

I start banging on the cineplex door with both fists, Thelma hanging on my back. "Somebody! Help!" But there's only the empty popcorn machine and the candy staring back through the window.

Effaline's flinging her skinny arms around, moaning and groaning like the possessed. "Come on, Effaline. Get up now." I coax her to her feet. "I'll be right back. Here. Hold Thelma. Thelma needs you."

Thelma needs no such thing, but I figure she'll take Effaline's mind off her misery long enough for me to try the back door.

The wind is howling mean. You can't hardly hear yourself crying for the fury of it. I stumble down the alley with the wind chasing me and throw myself against the back door. When nobody comes, I start kicking on it, screaming like a crazy person.

The door opens one little inch and a squinty eye peers out. "Jody?"

"Dooley!"

Well, like they say, never was I so glad to see a living person in this life. Poor Dooley almost drops his flashlight when I spill out Effaline's story. He hurries after me up the aisle into the lobby. The front door is rattling like cellophane. Dooley's fingers are shaking so bad he can't work his key. Effaline is out there wrapped around herself like bread dough ready to pop.

The door opens at last. It takes all Dooley's strength to hold on to it while I pull Effaline inside. She's shaking all over, hugging her arms to keep herself warm.

Her empty arms.

"Effaline? Where's Thelma?"

Effaline comes awake like a shot. "Thelma?" she shrieks. "Thelma!" She tries to push open the door, but I hang on to her. "I'll find her. You stay here."

A pain hits Effaline and she howls.

With Dooley's help, I push back out into the wind.

Thelma's not so dumb. She's gone only as far as the Walgreens and curled herself up in a planter. "Come on, Thelma," says I. "This storm will blow you clear to Texas."

It was so weird, just like Miss Thelma said. About the time that I get back to the cineplex, the hurricane stops dead. I look up at the sky, eerie and yellowish. Then I make a dash for the door.

It was the eye, looking for me.

Dooley and Effaline are right where I left them, like Gilligan survivors on the island. I ask them if they've called 911.

Dooley's gone into a zone.

Effaline's panting like a worn-out horse.

I stick Thelma onto Dooley. "Dooley, take Effaline into the theater. I'll call the emergency."

There is nothing deader than a dead phone, except maybe a house with a serial killer waiting in the bathroom. In times of emergency, knowing there are worse things can sometimes keep you thinking straight.

Word to the wise.

"Well, Jody," says I. "You've seen babies born before. It's nothing to be afraid of. It's the most natural thing in the world."

And on and on like that, while the phone receiver dangles dead from my hand.

Inside the theater, Effaline is laid out, her feet stuck straight over the seat in front.

Dooley's staring up at the ceiling like Chicken Little with his mouth open. We can hear the wind howling outside and things banging around, but we don't know what. A tornado could take the roof off a movie house, maybe a hurricane could, too.

"Dooley, I need you to find me some towels or some good clean rags. Can you do that?"

Dooley's great when you give him something to do, so I keep sending him for things. "Boil some water, Dooley. You know, in the coffeepot. Only don't put the coffee in."

He hands me the flashlight and runs off.

"And find some scissors!"

I wasn't exactly sure what the boiling water was for. But there's always all this calling for it when a baby's about to be born, so I was relieved that we would have some.

Meanwhile, Effaline is shrieking and howling like the wind herself.

I tell her to pant, like she was doing just before. "That's what you're supposed to do, Effaline. When you feel a pain coming, start panting."

Between us, we don't even have a watch to time the pains.

"It's coming!" cries Effaline.

"What? The pain or the baby?"

"I don't know! OOOOOOH! OOOOOWWW!"

Dooley comes back with the coffeepot in one hand and

scissors in the other. Thelma's looking down from his shoulder like the Snoopy vulture.

"Go to the lost and found, Dooley. Find some sweaters and coats. Something to lay down in the aisle."

"Why's Effaline screaming so bad?" he whimpers, wringing his hands.

I tell him the truth that nobody tells straight out like they should. "Because having a baby hurts, Dooley. It hurts ten times worse than the worst stomachache you ever had in your whole life. It's not one bit of fun."

Dooley runs off to the lost and found, happy to get away from stomachaches and Effaline's yelling.

Then she calms down some. "Hold my hand, Jody. I'm scared."

I take her hand and we sit there waiting for the next pain to hit.

Effaline says in a real little voice, "I didn't know it would be like this."

"What did you think it would be like?"

"I don't know," she says. "I thought about, like, having a baby. *Having* it, not doing this! I just thought about how nice it would be to have a baby all my own."

"Well, you're about to get one now," says I.

Things are quiet for a long time. I'm thinking about telling Dooley to tell the owner to buy one of them movie clocks that glow in the dark, just in case. But how many people are going to have their babies inside a movie theater?

It gave you something to ponder.

"I gotta go!" Effaline says all of a sudden. She tries to roll up out of her seat.

"Go where?"

"To the bathroom!"

"Okay! Okay! Let me help you."

Effaline runs hunched over like a beetle. I can hardly keep up with her.

Inside the ladies' she doesn't even make it to the stall. Down she goes onto the floor. "The baby's head is coming out! Jody! The baby's coming out! I can feel it!"

"Okay! Okay! It's all right. It's what's supposed to happen. Just lie still and breathe." I kneel down beside her.

Then comes the part you don't want to do unless you are a trained doctor. "Effaline, I gotta look, okay?"

"I don't care! Just get it out of me!"

Sweat is pouring off Effaline's face, which is red as a ripe tomato.

I help her wiggle out of her stretched-out underpants and, what do you know, she is right. There's a dark fuzz-ball trying to poke itself right out of Effaline. The beauty of the way it all works just takes your breath away. Only this isn't the time to stop breathing.

I whip off my T-shirt, which is all I have to put under her. "Push, Effaline! Push down!"

The door creaks open a hair. "Jody! Are you in there, Jody?"

"It's okay, Dooley. Bring the stuff."

Even then, scary as things were, I knew how hard it was

for Dooley to open the door to the ladies'. But he does. Like I say, you can count on him.

"Here's some coats," he says. "And here's some rags. The clean ones." He drops them in a pile and jumps back.

"Good job, Dooley. Now go watch at the front door, okay? If you see anybody, run right out and get help."

Well, there wasn't a chance of that, but I had to send him somewhere.

"Okay, Jody," he says, but his eyes are glued on the wet fuzzball that's still stuck where it was.

"God! Help!" cries Effaline, her eyes big as shiny silver dollars.

"Push, Effaline. You got to do it yourself."

"I can't! I can't!" She lays her head back down and starts thrashing about.

"Go, Dooley!"

Dooley goes out the door backwards.

I grab Effaline by the ears and stick my face right into hers. "Listen here, girl. I am only going to say this the one time. This baby is your doing and you're the one that has to get it born. Do you understand? Do you hear me, Effaline?"

"I hear you, Jody," she says, tears running off her face and down over my fingers.

"Then push!" I lay her head back down and get to the other end.

"Aaaagghhh!" groans Effaline, bearing down.

The fuzzball's wrinkly forehead comes sliding out, then the shut-tight eyes.

"Aaaagghhh!" groans Effaline, and out pops the whole head into my shaky hands.

"Go, girl! One more good push!" And out slides the whole danged baby, all its arms and legs where they need to be, sliding smooth as a greased pig.

Effaline's wailing and whooping like mad, but I can't attend to her. My hands have got a wet baby lying in them.

Then Effaline quiets down some. "What is it?" she says, and climbs up onto her elbows to get a peek.

"It's a little girl," says I.

But something's not right. The baby's supposed to be yelling her head off, mad as a hornet. I turn her over and pat her skinny little back a couple of times.

Nothing.

I pat it harder.

"Is she okay?" The baby's sac comes sliding out of Effaline in a rush. "Oooooh, ugh!" says Effaline. "Yuck!"

Then the baby lets out a howl that bounces around that ladies' like it was the Grand Canyon.

"She's fine," says I, real shaky. "She's just fine!"

I bundle the baby, still yelling and sticky with birth, in a nice soft cardigan sweater with pearl buttons and lay her on Effaline's chest. Already the tiny mouth is searching around for something to latch on to.

But if you know the very least about babies being born, you know there is one important thing left to do.

Even though I had seen my baby sister, Tamara, born and a cousin besides, I never did get a close-up look at the birthing cord. It is much fatter than you would expect.

Tough and rubbery as a garter snake. I pick up the scissors with scared, shaky fingers. I lay them back down. What if I cut Effaline and the baby apart and the baby starts leaking? How could I ever tie that fat slippery cord fast enough?

Would a regular old shoelace knot do, or was there some special doctor-kind they taught you in medical school?

Shoelace! With a prayer of thanks to whoever brought those Keds to the Hacienda, I pull out a shoelace. I tie it real tight down by the baby's end.

Just as I am about to cut the cord, the door bursts open to the prettiest starched blue shirt you have ever seen.

"Well, sugah, what have we got here?" says the paramedic, who is a black lady not a whole lot older than myself.

I find me a loose sweater to cover up with. And then I start into weeping and wailing, a little late, if you ask me, but it feels good and so I just go on like that while the paramedic checks out Effaline and the baby. Once I peek to watch the cord cut, easy as that.

The ladies' fills up with other blue shirts, then a stretcher. They lift Effaline right up onto that stretcher like she's nothing, the baby already sucking away, which it knows how to do without being told.

"Come with me, Jody!" Effaline yells, as they hustle her through the door.

We pass right by Dooley, Thelma curled up in his arms.

And that's how Cine gets born.

Of course, that's what Effaline named her. If you ask me, Cine's lucky she didn't get named for the commode.

Outside the cineplex, the world looked like King Kong had picked it up, given it a good shaking, and set it back upside down. Nothing was where it belonged. Cars turned all sideways in the middle of the street, store windows smashed, some roofs tore clean off. Rivers ran down the gutters. Wooden spoons, rubber sandals, and pacifiers were going along for the ride.

We got into the ambulance, all except for Dooley, who stood there shaking his head no. Then we drove off slow without the red light, since most everything that needed doing had got done already.

Dooley stayed there in the middle of the street, Thelma under one arm, the other one waving like we were never coming back.

"You're a hero!" I told Dooley later on.

"Like Spider-Man?"

"Yup. Like Spider-Man and Superman and Batman all rolled up into one."

If you think a person like Dooley is slow on the clutch, just you try to spot an ambulance in a hurricane. Sharonda, the paramedic lady, said Dooley was hollering louder than the wind and jumping up and down like a Mexican jumping bean.

After they got Effaline and Cine cleaned up and bedded down, a weary cloud came floating down on top of me. I could hardly stop myself from crawling into the bed beside Effaline's, which had another lady sleeping in it anyway. Effaline was conked out, too, so I left her be and headed home, hoping home would still be where I'd left it.

What Effaline would do with baby Cine was her own affair. I could tell her how to fix her hair or do her eyes, but no way was I going to make her keep a baby she didn't want. Pushing out a baby didn't make a person a mother any more than a wedding made a wife. There was a whole lot more to it than that.

I left that hospital, breathing down the cool fresh air. Tired as I was, what I felt mostly was strong. My hands that had done hundreds of dishes by then had worked a tiny miracle that day. One part of me said anybody would have done the same thing walking in my shoes, and that is true, but the other part said I had kept my head and done the best job anybody could have. I had helped bring a human being into this world, a little girl who might someday be the president, who could know?

I looked up at the clear blue sky, at the sun like a smile in the middle of it all, and I saw the hand of Fate: I was going to bring more babies into this world. I could be a paramedic, or a nurse, or even a baby doctor. No matter how long it took, how many years of school, how many dishes I would wash in the meanwhile, I was going to do it.

For better or worse, I had come a good long way from the altar and Bobby James Walker.

Sandyland Avenue had been hit hard. Some roofs were caved in and some were blown clear away. There was broken glass and trash all over the place. Thinking about Marilyn's beautiful furniture and my cherished Venice picture, I began to run at the corner, tripping over palm leaves and cereal boxes.

What do I see but one whole side gone off the Sandyland Apartments, so you could look inside and see how the people lived. It's a thing you don't see every day. I just stand there staring, my feet stuck to the sidewalk. People are putting what belongings they can find into piles, being kinder to each other than you would believe. They are even giving each other stuff, if they have extras. I go around meeting my neighbors for the first time, helping out where I can. How could I feel anything but guilty that number 11 is just as I had left it, with all its walls and not a thing touched.

Kirby is like a wild man let loose from a zoo. He scurries around, grabbing stuff and tossing it into the back of his pickup with the army colors and the gun racks.

He looks right through me like he'd never seen this face.

"Effaline's had her baby," says I, straight out. I don't want to believe he's Cine's real father, and maybe he isn't, but he probably has the right to know, in case.

"Huh," he says, not like a question but a dead-end thought. "Tell her I'm not taking none of her stuff."

He grabs up a Gators cap, sticks it on his head.

"Going someplace?"

"None of your beeswax."

"Well, who's going to run the place?"

"I don't know. You. You can do it. Here." He opens his

skinny wallet and finds a card inside. "This here's the owner. Tell her I got killed by the storm."

"But where are you going?"

"I don't know. Somewhere, nowhere, but not here. You can bet your sweet bippy I ain't going through another one of these!"

He jumps into his pickup.

"There goes child support," says I. But it goes without saying, he'd only be the deadbeat type.

He guns the engine and races off to nowhere, which is where he belongs, if you ask me.

*T*helma's Open 24-Hour Café and Grill was one of the lucky ones. It stood there proudly with all its taped-over windows, welcoming the police and the street workers with pots of good hot coffee. The dishes kept piling up but I didn't care. I just sang "Cielito Lindo" along with Enrique at the top of my voice. So what if I had got kicked out of the church choir for not carrying a tune right?

Then things started getting back to normal.

One day after Emma, Bertie caught me making the coleslaw.

"You've got to put more dressing in that," he said, hanging over my shoulder with his hands on his hips.

I shook in the poppy seeds. "Not this kind."

"What kind is that?"

"The Harris Teeter kind."

Well, I crossed my fingers in case I was lying. In all the commotion, I had not had five minutes together to check your deli case.

Still, you will be happy to know that Down-Home

Coleslaw made a name for me in Jackson Beach, and when Enrique went back to his Puerto Rican wife, I stepped in as a full-on cook.

But all that was later.

Two days after Emma, Effaline came walking home with Cine slung over her shoulder. She couldn't give her baby away, she said, no more than she could give a cat away. Which was at least better for baby Cine than finding herself in a Dumpster.

I took one long hard look at Effaline and another at baby Cine, who, no matter what Fate had in store, would always be a fully bonded part of my life. "Effaline," says I. "Guess what. You have got yourself a job."

"Job?" Like it's a word in the Arabian language.

"Come on," I said, grabbing her by the elbow. "Let's you and me get Cine laid down and figure out how this place runs."

The door to the office was blown open. Emma had left a mess, but that hardly changed the nature of the place. The manager's apartment wasn't touched, so you had to wonder whose things Kirby had made off with.

"Kirby said you could have the job, Effaline. He's gone for good. You are now a bona fide apartment manager."

"Me? But—"

"Don't worry. It's easy. All you do is collect the rent and tell people the plumber's coming any day now. It's easy. You'll see."

Well, I really didn't know, as you can tell. But Effaline

had to get on her own two feet, even if it took a hurricane to get her there.

I laid the card Kirby gave me on the counter and picked up the phone. That's when I saw that the owner lived in Dallas. When she answered the phone, the sound of her voice made me homesick.

I asked, in a low voice to make it sound older, "Is Mrs. Evans at home?"

"This is she. Who'm Ah speakin' to?"

It's finger-crossing time again. "Effaline . . ." In all that time I had not learned Effaline's last name.

"Podberry!" whispered Effaline.

"Potbelly?" I whispered back. "Potily," said I into the phone, shrugging my shoulders at Effaline. It's not my fault her name is so weird. "We have had a hurricane here, Mrs. Evans. I figured you should know."

"Well, yes, Ah do know," she said. Her voice was weak, like maybe she had used it a lot for about eighty years. "Ah have been tryin' to call Kirby."

"Well, Kirby's quit his job, Mrs. Evans. That's why I have stepped right in."

It was real quiet on the other end. "Is it real bad?"

I gave her a report, toning it down some in case her heart was bad.

"Well, if you think you can handle things . . ." She didn't sound too sure. More like she didn't have any other choice.

"You don't have to worry about one thing," I said.

She said there was insurance. Then she gave me a couple of numbers to call for the repairs. "They'll send me the bills," she said. "Are you sure you can handle this? What did you say your name was?"

Poor lady. What if I really was a criminal? But I guess she believed in the kindness of strangers, like I did.

My second call was collect to Mama. I knew she would be wild with worry and happy to accept the call. Tamara answered and wouldn't let go of me until Mama snatched the phone out of her hands.

"Mama? I'm fine. The hurricane never touched me!"

"What hurricane?" says Mama, which is the downside of having no TV and listening on the radio to the Bible stations only.

"You okay, Mama? Where's Daddy?"

"I'm fine, Jody. Don't you worry none about me."

Then she went on about Dora and Dina getting their hair chopped off just alike, and what Miz Hallahan in the next trailer over did after the cops came, and what she was making for the church picnic, no matter if the pastor's wife thought hers was the best pickled potato salad or not.

I had to ask from my heart, even when my brain said not to care. "I guess Bobby James's got him a new girlfriend already, huh?"

"Why, he came over just the other morning," Mama says. "Asking just as sweetly about you. I gave him your letter to read, I thought it only right, you being his wife and all."

"I'm not a wife anymore, Mama."

"You are in the eyes of God," Mama says. "In the eyes of Texas, too. Running off to Florida living the life of Riley doesn't change that fact, Sally Jo."

I could almost see Mama shaking her finger in my face, but I was truly not her little girl anymore, no more than I was Bobby James's wife. Blinded by the smile of a boy who could not keep a hold of his hands or his temper, I had made a girl's greatest mistake.

Like with that hurricane, I was just then starting to see how cleaning things up can be a whole lot harder than messing up in the first place.

"Tell Bobby James when you see him again that he can start the divorce papers, Mama. He can say I just run off, I don't care."

"Well, he's gonna write you. He tore the address off the envelope. You can tell him yourself."

Things were looking up at the Sandyland Apartments. Effaline would come running to me with every little question like I had the manager book with the answers in it, but she started to grow some confidence the way she'd grown that baby, without hardly a thought. A regular paycheck does wonders for a person's self of steam.

One day, I saw her out there bossing around the construction guys like she knew what she was talking about.

She was a good mother, too. Where she learned it, I will never know. Thelma acted put out for a while, then she gave up and moved in with me.

With Effaline's help, I did some deep-down cleaning and painting and general sprucing up. She didn't know how to do much, but she got into the spirit of it after a while.

Folks started moving in, handing over the first and last without even being asked. After a new carpet got put in number 12, two college fellas moved in there. The one, Phillip, is going to help me with my GED in trade for spaghetti dinners. I'm getting famous for spaghetti, too, only of course not with store-bought sauce.

It's in a quiet peaceful time, the kind when you are thinking how good your life is and storing up for the hard times, that I get the idea.

The repairs are finally done, it's my day off, and we are out by the pool. Effaline is setting out the stuff you need for a pedicure. When she sticks the toilet paper between my toes? That's when it comes to me.

"Effaline, we've got to have a party!"

"Cool," says Effaline. "Stick your foot in here."

I stick my foot in the dishpan full of Joy.

"We got lots of things to celebrate, Effaline." Then I think about that some. "Of course, the whole city does, but we can't invite everybody."

I go on thinking out loud, counting blessings on my fingers, while Effaline files my toenails down. "Baby Cine didn't choke on her cord. We both have jobs. We got a great place to live . . ."

I look proudly around at all we have done. Sandyland Apartments isn't hanging its head anymore.

Effaline frowns at my toenails, but she is always frowning about something.

"Pick up your head and look around this place, Effaline."

There were purple pansies in all the flower boxes, and every door was painted different. Ocean blue, asparagus, lime, pomegranate, plum, cotton candy, rose, banana, iris, tangerine, aquamarine, kiwi, or peachy pink, the exact color of a flamingo's wing. There were shiny gold numbers on the doors, too, and a new manager sign on the office with Effaline's name on it.

Effaline picks up her head. Her face has filled out some since Cine, and isn't near so pale. The way she got to do my toenails purple was by letting me do her eyes. I did them in lavender, instead of the pea green she likes so much. I could do them much better on other people than I could do them on me.

The first time I opened my shadow case since that fateful day at the Econo was when I did Effaline's eyes. For the longest time, my brain had worked that day at the picnic table like a nut, trying to figure out what all I done wrong. And then one morning while I was fixing my tea, it just came to me like that—nothing. I had nothing at all to be shamefilled about. I did not do one thing. And even if I did, no ifs, ands, or buts about it, Bobby James was the one who wronged me. He had no right to hit me.

I watch Effaline gazing around the place with her mouth a little open, like she's just getting it, too, what all we had done. "It was a lot of work, Jody," she says, with that little whine she has. "A whole lot of hard work."

"Yeah, but that's what's good, Effaline."

"Hard work?"

"Sure! Aren't you proud?"

A little sparkle comes into her blue eyes, and she lifts her chin some without meaning to. "Yeah," she says, grinning. "I guess I am."

"It'll be a thank-you party for Marilyn and a shower for the baby—"

"And a housewarming for us!" Effaline says. "We'll get presents."

I look at baby Cine under the umbrella table, waving her little hands in her laundry basket. "Cine could sure use a crib."

We planned the party every night for a whole week and then we sent out invitations, which took no time at all, as we did not know very many people.

The best part was ordering a bakery cake with all the names on it. Marilyn, for all the great furniture. Dooley, for saving the day. Effaline, for having baby Cine. Bertie, for giving me the cook job. And Miss Thelma for giving me a job in the first place. Effaline wanted to put Emma on there, but I said that was going too far. Then she said if it wasn't for Emma, we'd still have Kirby. So Emma went on there, too.

The bakery lady said that with all the names there'd be no room for the decorations. Then she said she'd stick some plastic flamingos on top and some other stuff, so we knew it would be perfect.

*O*n the night of the party, the Sandyland Apartments looked like Christmas, Halloween, Easter, and Valentine's Day all rolled into one. That's because you can find about every kind of decoration you want at a thrift store, and the Hacienda had them all.

Of course, we bought our supplies at your store, Mr. Teeter. Which is where I left the invitation, in case you didn't get it.

Marilyn's the first to show up. And does she look like a million bucks. She's wearing a black dress short enough to tug on, and her orange hair curls all down her shoulders.

The thing about a waitress uniform is, the minute you get out of it you look like a movie star.

"Here's the cake," says Marilyn, setting the box on the table. She had offered to pick it up on the way and wouldn't take a dime for it. As it was still taped up, I figured she didn't see her name yet. She thought the party was just a shower, like the invitation said.

"Bertie's bringing some stuff over in his pickup. You know, for the baby. A crib and stuff." She shrugs, her eyes the tiniest bit sad. Then she claps her hands together. "What can I do?"

I pour her some punch. "You can just relax right on your very own sofa," I say. "Everything is ready."

I had spent the whole day making finger foods, which is what you have to have. There were plates of sandwiches with the crusts cut off and Vienna sausages stuck with toothpicks. There were crackers with Cheez Whiz and enough deviled eggs for a county fair. Effaline made a bowl of green Jell-O with cottage cheese in it, which is what she grew up on.

Word to the wise.

What we didn't have was music, but Phyliss said she'd bring some, along with her husband, Big Al, who wouldn't miss a party for anything but a good gator hunt.

Bertie and Miss Thelma were the next to arrive. A man should never wear a bolo tie, but except for that, Bertie looks great. Even Miss Thelma has dolled herself up for the occasion with a Spanish shawl you could tell she thought highly of, as it smelled of careful packing away in mothballs.

You should have seen Bertie's face when he saw Marilyn in that black dress. Then he spots my Venice picture and goes over to it, like he doesn't want Marilyn to think he's ogling her too bad. "That's nice, Jody. Nice picture."

I tell him all about how Italy was my country, and how I always wanted to go there.

"You'll get there if you really want to," he says, his eyes going back to Marilyn as if they can't help themselves. "Set your heart on something bad enough, and you're bound to get it."

Dooley shows up looking like Dooley.

Effaline opens up her presents right away. This is fine, as Effaline is not good at waiting to get what she wants. Turns out, what she couldn't wait for was to see my face when I opened the cake box.

There in the middle of all those names, right square in the middle of that cake is JODY.

"Effaline!"

"Thanks, Jody," says Effaline. "Without you, me and Cine, well . . ." She shrugs and blinks back some real tears. She puts her arms around me with her butt stuck out, the way girls do. "You're my best friend in the whole world."

Everybody claps like mad. Then Phyliss puts some music on, the big band kind, which you can get into if you try real hard, and everybody starts dancing. It's a surprise to see Phyliss whirling around like that. Then I see that she's standing the whole time on Big Al's feet. It's a good marriage, you can tell.

But Dooley's the funnest one of all. He would come up to you and do this little bow, his face all serious. "May I have the pleasure of this dance?" he'd say every time, and wouldn't even notice how you were busting up. He knew how to dance that old-timey stuff, too. All us girls wore him out, taking turns.

After a time, baby Cine starts yelling louder than the big band. I tell Effaline that I'll get her. Effaline's dancing with Bertie. She hardly hears me. Uh-oh, says I to myself. By the things she told me, Effaline is a pretty fast worker. If Marilyn doesn't get busy, she is going to lose her chance at Bertie. And no matter what she said about men, she sure didn't wear that dress for Dooley or any of us girls.

I change Cine's diaper and stick her in a party dress with one of those bald-headed ribbon things. I lift her up out of her new crib. "Let's go to the party, baby girl."

To my great relief, Marilyn and Bertie are dancing to a slow number. Somebody has turned off the buffalo lamp, and so only the Christmas strings are lighting up the room.

Well, it's about as romantic as it gets.

I settle down in the rocker Marilyn brought for Effaline, with Cine on my shoulder. It's one of those perfect life-moments.

Then the front door opens and slaps against the wall.

"Where's my wife? Hey, Jody! You here?"

*E*verybody stops dancing.

Bobby James is holding on to the handle of the door he just walked through without knocking. Bobby James in his white James Dean T-shirt and his skinniest Wranglers. "Where is she?"

Then he sees me.

I can't move. Cine is nuzzling at my neck, even though she knows darn well I can't do her a lick of good.

Bobby James comes straight across the room without looking at another soul. Kneeling down in front of me, he grabs both chair arms. It's like he's caged me in that fast.

But he isn't looking at me. He's staring at Cine. "That's my baby, isn't it?" His eyes are brewing up a storm. "I knew it," he says. "I knew you were up to something."

"Jody?" Marilyn says.

"It's okay," I say, real quiet. "It's just Bobby James."

But I still can't move. Him and me are staring like a cat and a mouse.

I hear Bertie telling everybody that the party is over. They start moving a little toward the door, looking back over their shoulders.

"I'll be right outside," Marilyn says.

Bobby James stays right where he is, like we're the only two, well, three people in the room. He says in a quiet voice, "Did you name her after my mama, like we said?"

Well, you can't let a person know right off how stupid they are, at least not a person like Bobby James. "Bobby James," I say, not hardly knowing where to start. "This isn't your baby."

"Then whose is it?" He locks onto my arm, his fingers digging in.

Only a fool would notice how a boy's hair shines at a time like this. Or somebody who's still in love. Either way, it doesn't matter. She's still a fool.

"Take your hand off my arm, Bobby James."

"Tell me," he says, his jaw all fixed. But after one other hard squeeze, he takes his hand back.

"She's not yours or mine. She's Effaline's. How could we be having a baby? You can't grow a baby in four months."

"Who the hell is Ethaline?" he says.

"It's a long story," I say, hearing myself sigh like my own mama. "Keep your voice down. You're going to upset her."

I lift baby Cine off my shoulder. "Here. Hold her. I have to say goodbye to the folks." You would have thought I was handing him a mess of dirty laundry, but I knew he wouldn't drop her.

Nobody's going anywhere, as it turns out. They're camped in the deck chairs by the side of the pool. Marilyn and Effaline have clued them in. You can see it on their faces.

"Say the word," Bertie says, "and I'll send that boy right back to cattle country."

Marilyn takes his hand. She cradles it in her lap, smiling into his eyes. Which naturally takes every bit of fight right out of the man.

"Bobby James and me gotta talk sometime," I say. "Now's as good a time as any."

Big Al crosses his arms. "Well, we'll be right here," he says.

Bobby James comes out, baby Cine stuck straight in front of him. He's holding his breath, you can tell. I pass the baby over to Effaline. Then I pull up a chair for Bobby James and one for me.

For a while, everybody works at having a good country chat, but it's not all that it could be.

The whole time, Bobby James's knee is bouncing. When he plain can't stand it anymore, he nudges my arm and whispers into my neck, "Let's us take a ride."

Which is what he said on Patsy Cline Night. Just like that, like a tease, or a dare, with that crooked grin that could not be better even if it wasn't

That little voice inside me? Well, it's yelling like Cine with a diaper rash, No way.

He sits back. His foot starts tapping again. His gum cracks a couple of times.

All the lovebirds have gone inside to dance. Miss Thelma's snoring, her head flung back.

You should have seen Miss Thelma's face when she saw her name on that cake. If you thought I was surprised! She kept going over to the table and sneaking peeks at it, like she couldn't believe it was there.

Effaline's feeding Cine with that dreamy little smile.

Bobby James grabs my arm, this time soft. "I want to be with you, Jody. Alone. Come on! Please?"

All the times I missed him come flooding in, drowning out my little voice.

He takes my hand. "Let's just go sit in the car. Like we used to. We don't have to go nowhere."

My hand feels so right in his hand, like it has never washed a dish or painted a door or delivered a baby.

I tell Effaline we'll be back in a little while.

She wakes right up. Baby Cine pops off the nipple. "Where are you going?"

"Jody!" Dooley says, his mouth full of thirds on the cake. "Where are you going?"

"No place. Just out in the car. To talk. It's okay."

"I don't know . . ." Effaline says. She frowns just like a mother, which is what she is.

"We'll be right back. Promise."

"Well, okay," she says, but she doesn't look happy about it.

The Duster with its dented-in door has that look of waiting to it. We go around to Bobby James's side, his hand on my back, prom style. He leans over and opens the door. I climb in. There's Saint Christopher hanging from the mirror like always and a pack of Big Red on the dash. My heart's hammering like all bejesus as Bobby James slides into his seat.

I just can't help how that car smells like home.

He sighs, giving his head a little shake, like there is something working his mind.

I say what's true and not true, both at the same time. "It's good to see you, Bobby James."

He smiles his crooked smile. "Betcha thought you'd never see me again, huh?"

"Sometimes."

He reaches for the Big Red, unwraps himself a stick. "That your place? That one where the party is?"

"Yup. Number 11."

"Nice little place," he says.

"Well, it's not my furniture. It's on loan."

I think of all that's happened since that day in Perdido, and how hard it would be to explain to Bobby James. But he was bound not to listen anyway.

"Still," he says, "it's a nice place. Beats a double-wide." He drums the steering wheel with his thumbs. "Probably can't have dogs, though. Right?"

Crack, crack goes that gum.

I don't get what he's driving at.

"I don't think so. Why?"

"Why?" His eyebrows go straight up, like I have surprised him near to death. "What about Pete and Repeat?"

"The dogs?"

They were his dogs, but after living with them in the Duster for thirteen weeks they were sort of mine, too.

He looks around me at the door to number 11. "We could sneak them in."

A sick feeling takes me over like the flu. "You brought your stuff with you? You're staying?"

"Just my stereo and the guns. I'll have to go back for the dogs. Course I'm staying. What didja think?"

I don't know where to start. The words won't line themselves up right.

Bobby James fiddles with the wheel. "How come you never wrote me, Jody?"

I swallow some dry spit. It feels like I could look right in that rearview mirror and see my eye, all busted up, just like it was.

"You hurt me, Bobby James."

It isn't a laugh exactly, but it's close. "Aw, Jody! I didn't mean to leave you, girl. You just made me mad, staying in that bathroom like you weren't never coming out."

He doesn't even remember. Sometimes when I get real tired I can still feel my eye, and he doesn't even remember it.

"Come over here," he says, tugging on my arm. "You been missing me?"

The thing is, you don't remember just the bad times. That would make it easy. There were all those nights in the Duster backseat, before Perdido, when Bobby James would curl around me like a shell. I had never slept so sweet.

"Well, sure, I missed you."

He slings his arm over my shoulders and pulls me tight. I wiggle loose a little to breathe. He snuggles me back. I settle my head against his shoulder, and the next minute, we're kissing.

It's like I can't help myself, no more than a baby with a cookie.

We break apart after a while, the both of us breathing fast. Bobby James looks past my shoulder out at the Sandyland patio. "They ever gonna leave? I want me a good time with my wife!" He winks like that bad preacher we had for a while at the Purley Baptist.

I brush the tears off my face. "They'll leave after a while, I guess."

"Her, too?"

"Who?"

"The one with the baby."

"Effaline? Oh, not for a while." That's when I know for dead sure it's only the kissing that I want.

"She living with you?"

I cross my fingers where he can't see them. "Yeah. Her and baby Cine."

He spits a cuss word and pushes me away. Then he reaches for the keys and starts that big engine. I yell and grab his arm, but he stomps the gas and we go fishtailing out onto the street.

"Bobby James, stop this car right now!" I turn my head and watch the lights of the Sandyland Apartments shrinking in the black smoke behind us like a dream.

Bobby James cranks the wheel left, stomps the gas, and runs straight through a stop sign.

"STOP THIS CAR!" We are heading for the highway. I can see it up ahead through my whipping-around hair, just a few cars this time of night, the road lit up like a creep-show movie.

I make a grab for the keys, but his hand locks onto my wrist like a handcuff. "Be still!" he says. "You want to wreck the car?"

"Take me home!"

"Where's home, Jody? Do you even know where home is? You're my wife. You shouldn'ta taken off that ring. How do you suppose that makes me feel?" He tightens his hand on my wrist. "Like two cents. That's how." Then he throws my hand back at me.

We're racing straight down the freeway into the dark, Bobby James carrying on with this and that, how it was all my fault, how I wasn't no better than my mama, for all her good deeds at the church.

"Your old man? You were always telling me stories about him. But, Jody? I worked with the man. He's a stand-up guy."

The world looks cracked through the bad window on my side. I tell Bobby James what he already knows. "Daddy's been smacking Mama around since I was in dia-pers, Bobby James. Even before that."

"Well," he says, shaking his head, "she probably asked for it."

I watch the flat weedy ground flying by. The moon's as full as it's going to get, hanging plump and ripe as a grapefruit. I think about Effaline, how she'd have made a run inside when we took off. Would she call the cops? And if she did, so what? Bobby James was my legal husband. He had a right to me.

"Slow down, Bobby James. There's no need to be going so fast."

"Did I ask for your two cents?"

There's that two cents again.

"Where are we going?"

"Someplace," he says. "Someplace we can be alone."

Not a tree or a house in sight, just the moon shining down like a spotlight in a prison yard.

I swallow my heart down and say real calm, "They're probably all gone by now. We can go back to my place."

"Yours and that Ethaline's. No, thanks."

"I can tell her to—"

"Will you shut up, Jody? Just shut your damned mouth. All I been hearing in my head since I left you at the gas station is you telling me what to do. Well, I'm finished with that. Understand?"

I lay my head back against the seat, the tears streaming down my face.

He grabs my thigh and digs in hard. "Understand?"

"I understand."

"I got things to say to you, and you're going to listen if I gotta smack you. Understand?"

That was when I'd have thrown myself out of that car if I could, but because of that door, I was locked in there tighter than a Houdini box.

We zip past what few cars are on the road like they are crawling. I think about writing HELP on the window with lipstick, but I have come away without my bag. And I know it would only make Bobby James madder. Already he's working his jaw the way he does before the worst.

The wind is screaming through his open window, blowing his dark hair every which way. Eighty-five, almost ninety miles an hour. He has to yell over the wind to make me hear. "I love you, Jody. That's the main thing I got to say. I love you. You are my awful wedded wife. Just like that preacher said, till death do us part. Did you forget that?"

Ninety-five, almost a hundred.

The siren comes from a long way off. At first, Bobby James doesn't hear it, still going on about us like he really does love me. Only I know it's just words.

"What the—" He looks in his mirror and blue light washes across his face. I turn and watch the cop car coming on, blue light twirling, siren going to beat the band.

Bobby James says the worst cuss word then. Says it again and punches the steering wheel with his fist. But he lets off that gas and the Duster starts winding down.

"Get me my license," he says when we are parked by the side of the road. "In there." He runs his fingers back through his hair, real nervous, like there's things that I don't know about, some trouble he's already in.

I open the glove box and hand him his wallet.

A voice tunnels in from a long way off. "Step out of the car and put your hands on the hood."

Bobby James looks over at me like he's about to cry, like he's about ten years old. "See? See?"

Well, I didn't see, but what could you say?

He gets out of the car and does like he's told. I watch him through the windshield, hunched over, his T-shirt white as brand-new. He does the funniest thing then. He looks straight at me and smiles. It's a gentle thing, like his smile when he asked me to dance that very first time.

A light shines into my face, making me blind. "You all right, miss?"

I am not all right. I know I'm going to be, but I am not all right. My heart has sprung a bad leak.

"Yes, sir."

"You sure?"

"Yes, sir."

"You got some ID?"

"No, sir. Not with me."

"He says you're his wife. Is that right?"

"Yes, sir. Yes, sir, I am."

He takes the light away. I watch him pat down Bobby James. Then he lets him stand just normal.

Bobby James gets back into the car. The cop writes the ticket and pushes it through the window for Bobby James to sign. "You slow down, son. If this was Texas, you'd be in jail. You know that?"

"Yes, sir."

We watch the cruiser drive off.

"You could have asked that cop for a ride," Bobby James says after a while.

"I could have."

"How come you didn't?" His voice is quiet, tired-sounding.

Out here it looks like the end of the world, like God ran clean out of ideas and closed up shop.

"I don't know, Bobby James. Except I do love you. You never did want to believe it, but it's true."

I have never seen him look so sad. I guess he was way ahead of me. "I'll take you on home," he says.

All the way, we're holding hands. Like we're fifty years old, with all that life sadness between us.

"Your daddy says he can get me a job with the mufflers."

"That's good."

"Think you'll ever come back home?"

"For a visit, sure."

After a while, he says, "You're not the way you used to be, Jody."

In the light from passing cars, it looks like Saint Christopher is winking at me, which of course he would not, being a saint.

"I guess not."

"You used to be, I don't know . . . *sweet*." He looks over to see how I'm taking it.

I almost say what I said that time to Kirby, but I think better of it.

"You're real changed."

I guess that about says it all.

We pull up to the curb at the Sandyland Apartments. All of the windows are dark except mine, where you can see the Christmas lights glowing inside.

Bobby James cuts the engine. "Your friend's waiting up for you, I guess."

"I guess."

"Will you write me, Jody? Like you do your mama and Jolene and them?"

"Sure I will."

Deep sigh. "Your suitcase is in the trunk. You want it?"

"Well, yeah!" This is like getting the wrong door on *The Price Is Right*, if you know what I mean. Still, you're glad you got the consolation for your time.

Bobby James opens the door and gets out. I climb out after him. We go around to the back of the Duster. He opens the trunk. There's all his stereo stuff and the hunting guns in their cases.

I want to touch him in the worst way. Just touch his shoulder or his cheek. Just for a minute. I can't hardly help myself, but I don't do it.

He pulls out my suitcase, still wrapped with the bungee cord, and pushes down the trunk lid to close it. Then he walks me to my door, like we have just come back from a long, long trip. A honeymoon that didn't work out.

He hands me my suitcase. "Be good," he says.

"I will. You be good, too."

"I'm always good," he says with his crooked smile. "I'm the man." It's a joke we had between us once.

He reaches over and tugs a little on a piece of my hair, thinking I don't know what, and then he turns away.

I watch until the Duster lights are two tiny red dots in the dark.

*B*ertie unwraps the little wire thingie from around the cork.

"Careful, don't shake it!" Effaline says, hanging on to the sides of the basket, her pale face greenish. Above us is the biggest red-and-yellow balloon I have ever seen, and the bluest blue sky. Counting Texas.

Bertie pulls at the cork but it won't come out.

"Here, let me," Marilyn says. She holds the bottle between her thighs and gives that cork the good old waitress pull. Out it pops, along with a big gush of bubbles. She pours us each a cup. Her brand-new engagement ring sparkles like the real thing, which maybe it is.

I hold up my Dixie cup. "Here's to Bertie and Marilyn!"

Cine lets out a big burp. Everybody laughs. Dooley pats her back like mad.

We all clink our cups, which don't exactly clink. But you can't have glass on a hot-air balloon, and what's the difference anyway? Like they say, it's the insides that count.

The sun has just gotten itself up, so everything looks golden, our faces and hands, even the freeways and trailer parks way down below us. I hang over the side and it's just like flying.

"Hey, Jody," Bertie says, "want to go to Venice?"

"You bet!"

That balloon does not scare me one bit. I'd have gone anyplace that thing would take us.

The same could not be said for Effaline or Dooley, whose eyes are big as they'd be in a fun house the whole time.

Fire whooshes up and the balloon goes higher, taking our stomachs with it. We sail straight over the coast of Florida, over that swimming-pool-blue water, and the highway that goes as long as you're willing. We pass a bunch of pelicans all in a line, beating their wings real slow.

"What if a bird pecks the balloon?" Effaline squeaks. "What if he makes a hole in the balloon?"

Bertie explains how tough the balloon is, what it's made out of and all that mechanical stuff. But Effaline does not look any better for knowing.

"There it is, Jody," Bertie says after a while, pointing down. "There's Venice."

I look at where he's pointing but all I can see is roofs and roads and swimming pools, same as before.

Well, I knew it wasn't Italy. Even I knew that.

Still.

"Venice, Florida," Bertie says. "There's one in California, too, only that one has real canals."

"They should at least build them a blue dome," says I, "if that's what they're going to call it."

Thing is, not everything is what you expect. Not jobs or hurricanes or coleslaw or movies, and surely not husbands. But not to worry. You pull yourself up, dust yourself off, and keep on going. Then one day? Well, you open your eyes a little bit wider and there's the doors all painted, friends everywhere, and a baby drops into your hands. It's a miracle.

"Well, at least you can say you've been to Venice," Bertie says.

With his arm around Marilyn and that balloon over his head, Bertie looks like the world's happiest man. "Hey, Dooley," he says, "would you like to go to Disney World?"

Dooley thinks about that for a minute. "Okay," he says, but he doesn't look happy.

"They've got Ferris wheels, Dooley," I tell him. "Better than Ferris wheels."

"Okay, Jody."

Ferris wheels are plenty high enough for Dooley. You can tell without him saying it.

Fire whooshes up into that big balloon and we sail off through the blue, blue sky, not a cloud in sight.

Well, I have surely tried your patience, Mr. Teeter, going on the way I am bound to do. I was going to get to the point about the coleslaw half a dozen times, but then I'd think of something else and go running off with that.

Thing is, Down-Home Coleslaw is public property now. You probably saw it in the *Jackson Beach Sun Times* Sunday food section, along with my picture for being the winner. Now any old person can have it, so you might as well stick with your own.

Coleslaw's like a lot of things in life, when you think about it. It's something you want so bad sometimes, you can go plain crazy. But the next day? You kind of wonder why you craved it in the first place.

You probably want to know what happened to Bobby James.

Not long after the balloon ride, I got a sympathy card from my mama.

Dearest Daughter,

I hope this letter finds you in good spirits as I have some real bad news for you. What they're saying down at the Baptist is that Bobby James has took up with another woman, the winner of the same contest as you, the Miss Congealiality, only the year after. Which put my mind to thinking the man still loves you, what with him picking the same girl twice like that. Daddy and him are working pretty steady with the mufflers, so it's not too late for you to have things the way you want them right here in Purley. In case you are wondering why the sympathy, it was all I could find without going out to the store. Write soon.

Your loving mother

Well, my heart stopped and started a couple times reading that letter. Part of me wanted to run straight back to

Purley and snatch Bobby James right out of that girl's hands, but the other part's the part with the good sense. That part went right on doing what was smart and right for

Yours Very Truly,

Sally Jo Walker (Jody)